Quixote
Twisted Tales of Familiar Faces
Stephen Wertzbaugher

M4L Publishing

Francisco Javier de Cervantes

Argent light from the full moon shone through an uncurtained window, painting my six-year-old Dulcinea's bedroom corner with threads of silver-spun silk. Night's shadows bathed the rough-hewn cedar walls and shaded the coarse cotton curtain sewn by my wife, Nayara, that hung against the doorpost.

A fire crackled in the hearth, the scents of oak, juniper, and pine tickling our noses. Outside, the evening winter breeze brushed glass and timber with icy pellets, tapping a staccato beat against the window, chased by the peaceful bleating of our sheep. Heat from the fire snuggled our bodies as I prepared to put our daughter to bed.

Dulcinea giggled, the spirited soprano cadence of her childish voice dancing alongside the firelight as I lifted her to my shoulders. She hugged my neck, her joyous laughter tugging a reluctant smile from my wife, distracting her from her sewing.

Nayara winced, her usually nimble fingers stumbling as they wrenched needle and thread through the unbleached muslin she'd procured for a new apron. Worry creased her brow. She glanced up at us, disapproval masking her usual indulgent look.

"Put the girl to bed, Francisco, please. It is past her bedtime and the hour grows late." She patted the seat cushion beside her. "And you said you would sit with me this evening while I sew."

"But, Momma," Dulcinea protested. "Pappa promised to read *Don Quixote* to me tonight." She leaned over my shoulder. "You promised you would read to me tonight, Pappa."

"And I will keep my promise. Tonight, we shall continue the story of the grandest and most chivalrous knight to have ever lived."

Dulcinea clapped her hands.

Nayara brushed me with a reproving look. "Francisco, you spoil the child."

I shrugged, tickling the bottoms of my daughter's feet. She screamed with delight, kicking and wriggling her toes. "But I promised the child," I said. "And you know how she loves the tales of Don Quixote."

"Fine," Nayara said. She waved away my excuses. "Off with you. But do not dawdle."

Pretending to be her horse, I pranced into her sleeping corner and laid her into the welcoming folds of a worn-down comforter. I retrieved *Don Quixote* from the shelf above the alcove entry, seated myself beside her bed. She stared at me, eyes wide with innocence and wonder as I stroked the frayed leather binding.

"Have I told you the story of how our family came to own such a treasure?"

"Yes, Pappa, you have," she replied. "And when it is my time, you shall grant me the honor of possessing it after you."

I tweaked her button nose and kissed her forehead. "You have been listening to the adults too much," I said as I opened the book. The weary binding creaked like old bones, aged parchment rustling in the quiet as I turned the pages, running my fingers along the pitted surface, tips memorizing each pen stroke scratched into the vellum. "Shall I begin?"

She yawned and nodded, her eyes beginning to droop, a contented smile curling her delicate lips.

Five minutes later, I closed the book, winced at the rasping of leather against parchment. When would I have the binding repaired and so preserve Dulcinea's inheritance? There never seemed to be time. I stood. Nayara lounged where I had abandoned her, intent upon her needle and thread as she darned a pair of my worn socks. I sat beside her and kissed her cheek.

She smiled. "Apology accepted."

Golden firelight danced through her silver-streaked raven hair.

"Is she asleep?"

"Yes, my love."

"You indulge the child too much."

"How can I not?" I said. "She is our only one."

Nayara set down her sewing, took my hand and placed it over her stomach. "Not for much longer."

I gaped at her, dumbfounded. Had I heard her rightly? Were we to be parents once more? After grieving the loss of two others? "Truly?"

She nodded, cupped my chin in her hand, and kissed my lips. "Yes, my love. La Virgen María has granted our prayers and blessed us with yet another chance to be parents. The little one shall join our family in seven months."

I laughed, sprang to my feet, pulling Nayara with me. She pretended to resist, surrendered to my ardent embrace and tender kiss, smiling and giggling like the schoolgirl I had fallen in love with fifteen years earlier in La Mancha.

"We must celebrate!"

"Shush," she scolded. "You will wake Dulcinea."

One of our herd dogs barked. Its urgent snarls joined a moment later by a second and a third of our dogs. The sheep took up the dog's cries, their bleating growing anxious and unsettled.

The wind rattled the front door. Threads of smoke from outside slid through the seams, gathering in a haze at the threshold.

I untangled myself from Nayara, put an ear to the door.

Three distant, rapid gunshots echoed through the night. A dog yelped, fell silent. The second dog bayed, the volume of its dissonant caterwauling receding into oblivion.

I swore under my breath, loaded my shotgun, stepped to the door.

"Francisco?" Nayara said, her voice trembling, edged with foreboding.

I looked back at her.

She stared, terror mingled with anger glinting behind her velvet brown eyes, hands worrying at her stomach. "You promised the cattlemen would leave us alone." She clenched her fists, arrows of defiance aimed at my foolish recalcitrance. "You swore it!"

Had we the time, I would have begged her forgiveness for my hubris. "Bar the door behind me. Take Dulcinea into the root cellar. Stay with her. Do not come out."

She did not move. "You said their article in the newspaper would come to nothing." Anguish twisted her expression. "You promised!"

I flinched, the distress writhing through her voice crushing my heart. "Do as I say. Now!"

I did not wait to see if she obeyed, but strode into the frosted chill of the night, yanking the door closed behind me. Moonlight cut a silver swath across the sky, blanched the starlight piercing the velvet ether. The biting winter wind snapped at my coat collar, ruffling the brim of my hat as I stepped to the edge of our porch, searching the gloom. Flickering yellow light glowered through the window behind me. White-gray wood smoke trailed from the chimney, twirling and twisting in the wind, forming a dingy halo above me.

The silhouette of the grizzled and hoary mountain mahogany that bordered our farmyard stood tall and silent. An owl hooted from an upper branch, masked behind a thick veil of leathery and sticky dark green leaves, a quiet countermelody to the restless complaining of the sheep.

Our dogs were quiet.

I cocked back the hammers of my shotgun, held it ready, and waited.

Distant, rumbling thunder shivered the air.

I stared into the night, my heart thumping, my breath rasping in my ears.

The glow of torches lit the night. The porch throbbed beneath me. Lightning flashed, illuminating the ragged tops of the mountains.

Four riders materialized, reining their lathered horses to a troubled stop several paces away. Empty flour sacks covered their faces, holes sliced through the canvas for eyes and mouths, hats crammed down on their heads to anchor the makeshift hoods so they would not skew in the wind. They held torches, jittery flames dancing upon their sooty poles, oily black smoke roiling into the air.

Despite their clumsy attempts to disguise themselves, I knew these men. Knew the brands scorched into the flanks of their mounts. Knew the hatred and derision blazing from their cloaked eyes. Cattlemen. Ruby Creek town founders. Come west to settle the prairie, drive out the original inhabitants, and carve legacies for themselves and their descendants. Civilized men, yearning to bring their ideals of culture to the wilds, no matter the cost. Or despite it.

Hard, coarse men wearing the thin veneer of couth, cultivation, polish, and refinement. Men that despised sheepmen more than they hated the Indian.

I raised my shotgun. "I do not wish any trouble this evening," I said. "Both my wife and daughter are abed for the night, and I would hope not to disturb their slumber."

The lead rider urged his horse ahead, curbed the animal when it balked. "You were warned not to bring your vermin across the border into our territory, Cervantes." He leaned forward, his mount skipping from side to side. "You were informed of the consequences if you chose to do so."

I lifted my chin in defiance, moved my finger over a trigger. "I read the spurious article you published, warning us not to venture into Colorado, Daugherty."

He straightened, his free hand hovering over the butt of his pistol.

"Yes, I know you, Tristan Daugherty. As I know your fellows." I faced each, shouting their names back at them. "Henry McMillan. Joseph Pellerman. Sherman Barrett." I turned to Daugherty. "Tristan Daugherty." I raised my voice above the rising clamor from the milling sheep. "Is not the prairie for everyone who so chooses to raise stock and a family?"

"For cattle, yes," Daugherty said. "Not for the stinking beasts you've brought. Not for the locusts that will strip the range of everything before moving on, leaving nothing behind but dirt, poverty, and starvation." He sat upright in his saddle. "But we are not barbarians," he said. "We'll give you an hour to gather your family and what possessions you can carry and leave."

"And my sheep?"

He blurted a low, throaty chuckle that stroked the hackles on the back of my neck.

"You should have considered their fate before you brought them from Wyoming into Colorado."

Wood groaned behind me.

I turned.

Nayara stood within the yawning maw of our threshold, my pistol clasped in her trembling hands, the barrel swinging drunkenly in the lamplight.

She cocked back the hammer, cried, "Leave us alone!"

A horse screamed and reared.

Nayara flinched.

Gunshots exploded. Wood splintered around Nayara. She jerked backward, arms flailing, the pistol flying from her grasp as she disappeared through the doorway.

I howled.

Burning agony ripped through my side, spinning me like a top. I stumbled a step, pinwheeled the shotgun at the riders, pulled both triggers. Thunder roared, driving me from my feet, slamming me into the wall. I crumpled, shaking hands, trying to reload the weapon, fumbling shells, fingers scrambling to retrieve them as they rolled out of reach.

Men shouted.

Horses screamed.

Gunshots detonated through the air.

A burning coal oil lantern sailed through the night. It smashed through a window, raining glittering slivers upon my head, slicing my face.

An eye blink later, a firestorm erupted.

A rope dropped around my chest and snapped me from the porch, dragging me into the dirt.

Fire roared, flames lacerating the sky, clawing at summer dried cedar and pine, pooling and spreading outward in hot, flickering patterns, washing over boards, climbing walls, and gorging on the timber. It swirled stinging dark gray smoke into the night, throwing glittering sparks in its wake.

I screamed, struggling against the hemp that crushed my arms to my sides. An iron-shod hoof slammed down on my leg, slicing through flesh and crushing bone.

Agony slashed through me. I fell back, teeth grinding, my shriek plastered to the roof of my mouth, throat constricted, voice pulverized.

I could do nothing but watch, my body clenched by the horror erupting around me. "Dulcinea," I howled into the dirt.

"Bring him," Daugherty said, his voice dripping malice.

The rope tightened, jerked, and dragged me across the trampled ground. They heaved me against the gnarled and calloused trunk of the mountain mahogany, its leafy branches yearning toward the brooding moon.

A deeper darkness blotted out the surging flames.

A horse snorted.

Leather creaked.

The slap of boots against the hard pack.

The crunch of approaching footsteps.

A hooded nightmare filled my world, breath stinking of rancid tobacco and cheap whiskey. Tristan Daugherty.

Fingers curling into my shirt collar, yanking me forward to gape into dark, soulless eyes.

"You should have stayed in Wyoming," Daugherty said.

My stomach clenched, fingernails gouging bloody holes in my palms as I watched the inferno annihilate my hope. "You should not have murdered my family," I whispered, my voice laced with venom.

He backhanded me.

I spat blood into his face, drove my uninjured foot between his legs.

He dropped me, cursing, and drawing his pistol, slammed it into the side of my head, followed by a boot to my ribs.

Hands fisted into my hair, pulled me upright. Daugherty's face twisted with malignancy.

"I shall have my justice," I said.

Daugherty's eyes narrowed. "Brazen words. But without teeth."

Daugherty turned. "Let him watch, then hang him. When it's done, let his corpse smolder with the charred bones of his family."

The rope double-looped around my neck, squeezed until I sputtered and choked, was tossed over an overhanging branch, the hemp scraping across chafing bark. The slack vanished, crushing my windpipe as I was hauled skyward. My feet dangled and kicked, my jerking body twirling. My chest heaved, drank oblivion, my eyes bulging from their sockets. My tongue licked the air, hands yanking at the noose and tearing flesh from my fingertips.

My mind constricted, thoughts strangled, their final moments screaming, "Justice," before shriveling and dying.

Startling, piercing agony drove through my skull.

Dimly remembered sunlight.

I woke.

Heat licked my soot-soaked flesh.

I lay in ash and charcoal at the pinnacle of a funeral pyre, my bones blackened, skin bubbled and blistered, clothes tattered, the edges licked by the smoldering coals.

Phantoms stumbled through my mind, sluggish, their gait awkward and infantile. A child's face materialized, her flesh melted from her charred skull, jaw contorted into a hideous shriek, liquid eyes oozing from filthy and foul sockets.

My hand slipped into my gaping chest, touched...nothing.

I did not breathe. And yet awareness clung to my scattered thoughts, whipping them into a boiling frenzy. A keening wail rose, spewing grief and rage into the empty chaos.

I dug bony fingers into the scalded ruin. They scraped scorched leather, seared parchment. Whispered voices wriggled into my thoughts. Images flashed, paraded lewd figures across my mind. Corruption, depravity, and perversion of innocence.

A murmured name. "Dulcinea."

The flicker of extinct tears upon my heat-shriveled flesh. "Dulcinea," I muttered into the emptiness. Taken from me, robbed of her innocence by tempestuous, degenerate, and depraved monsters disguising themselves as men of honor, integrity, and justice.

Another shriek scaled the clinging murk, echoed across the oblivion.

I dragged my hand from the ruin upon which I sat. It clutched a book, the leather binding burned and blackened, the pages curled and pitch-dark, the ink tarred, words maligned by the heat of hell. I stared into its depths.

Another name was spoken through cracked and split lips. "Quixote."

Followed by the words, "Justice and honor." They flowed from the book clasped in my clawed hand.

"Daugherty. McMillan. Pellerman. Barrett," I croaked.

The names became scribed with fire into the seared parchment.

"Flesh for flesh. Tooth for tooth. Eye for eye."

"For Dulcinea," the pages murmured. "Until the end of things."

I nodded, flesh-less fingers caressing the brittle pages.

Silence enveloped me. The wind scoured my flesh, tugged at the ruin of my hair. A shiver galloped through my devastated body.

Quixote. Knight errant. Seeker of Truth. Harbinger of Justice and Honor.

For Dulcinea. My unborn child. And Nayara.

Daugherty. McMillan. Pellerman. Barrett.

Their names and faces scorched into my mind and burned into the pages of my book.

The sun rose above the mountain peaks, searing away the night.

I chiseled a hole into the frozen ground, laid the burnt bones of my gentle Dulcinea beside the remains of her mother, the grave unmarked, and mumbled prayers I no longer believed in.

Then, clutching the book to my incinerated chest, I staggered into the wilderness.

Emerson Daugherty

I could hear Daddy and Mommy screaming at each other from their bedroom down the hall.

Glass shattered and something heavy slammed into a wall, shaking the corner of my room where I huddled. I clutched the phone from their bedroom to my chest, hands shaking as I tried to dial the emergency number.

More glass smashed into a wall.

I dropped the phone, clamped a hand over my mouth.

Daddy and Mommy were calling each other bad names and yelling, their voices echoing through the upstairs.

I grabbed the phone from between my feet, hesitated. What was the emergency number? And then I remembered. I pressed the buttons.

"9-1-1. What's your emergency?"

"Hello? Help. I need help. My daddy and mommy are yelling at each other, and I'm afraid."

My closet door creaked open.

I gasped, dropped the phone.

The gloomy light clawed at toys scattered over my bedroom floor. Long, splintery fingers reached toward me from the edges of my bedroom, where the light from my Barbie lamps couldn't reach. From the back of my closet, red, glowing eyes stared at me, and I heard the sound of smacking lips.

Clenching my mouth closed, I bit my bottom lip, squeezed my eyes shut. I pressed myself into the corner between my desk and the wall, hugging my knees, trying not to cry, the rough surface scratching my back, making my skin itch and crawl with ants. The phone lay on the floor under my legs. I heard voices, their sounds tiny and far away. I wanted to pick up the phone, but when I reached for it, an icy hand stroked my cheek, slipped a creeping chill between my ribs, caressed my heart, gorged my chest with bitter, cold-blooded breath.

I gasped, squirmed further into the wall, sobs blubbering from my gaping mouth, my hands swatting at the shimmering air, slapping the groping claws from my skin. Tears ran down my cheeks, mixed with the snot running from my nose.

My bedroom window stood open to the moonless night, the gauzy, frilly curtains Mommy had bought me flapping like toddler ballerinas in the breeze. Snowflakes floated through the gaps. White and bunny fluffy, they fluttered on the cool air for a breath before falling to their deaths on my pillow and bedspread.

I squeezed my eyes closed, slapped my hands against my ears, tried to pretend the shouts and screams battering the upstairs came from one of Daddy's scary movies and not from him and Mommy.

Silence tore through my panic, almost shoved me through the wall. I opened my eyes, held my breath, shaking.

The air in my bedroom grew thick and hot. I sucked in a heavy breath. For an instant, the window curtains shuddered, then fell limp and dead against the windowpane. The wind tickled the edges, shoved a few scrambling flakes past the twitching seams before it ran away.

Daddy screamed. Mommy screamed back.

The glowing eyes peeking out at me from the back of my closet blinked, snuffed out, leaving coal-black darkness behind. I shook my head, mumbling a half-remembered prayer my daddy had taught me when I was little. He told me the words would keep the monsters away. I didn't remember if they worked then. They didn't work now.

Whispers slid through the struggling light in my room, the sounds sharp and stinging, like the edge of my daddy's knife when I had taken it without his permission and cut my hand. I had cried then. I couldn't cry now. The tears were stuffed too far down, trampled by a booted foot that I shouldn't have been able to see.

A sudden explosion ripped through the upstairs.

I jumped, cried out, crawled from my corner to the side of my bed, where I burrowed between the wall and the dark wooden frame hugging the mattress, shaking, beginning to vomit the sobs from the bottom of my tummy.

Another explosion smacked my ears, made me cringe. Made me wish I could be invisible and not the pretend kind I played with Daddy before I grew too big for those kinds of games.

Sluggish footsteps scuffed across the wood floor from the direction of Daddy and Mommy's bedroom. Mommy's high-pitched voice sang a made-up song, the words slurred and clumsy like the way she talked after drinking too much of her grape juice, which seemed to happen a lot since Daddy became boss of the town. Her voice crept down the hallway toward my room, her made-up words scratching and scraping against my brain.

A chorus of whispered voices joined hers, their tune off-key and jagged like the broken edge of a rock from our backyard. Ghosts swam through the air in front of me. Some came close, their faces melted like wax from a candle, their eyes glowing red and orange. They flickered, squiggly and irregular. I bit my tongue, tried to crawl into the wall, pushing against my back. One face broke away from the rest and came close. Thin as a stick, with black and silver whiskers that drooped down from the chin in a waterfall of crinkled hair. The nose looked like the handle of one of our table knives. Stuck into the bottom of the flaring nostrils floated two long and skinny horse tails, the ends dancing and singing in the wind of the voices.

The face stopped, stuck its nose into my face, the eyes wide and wild, glinting with a terrifying glee. It smiled, the twiggy mouth showing two ragged and uneven rows of yellow teeth stained with something gooey and red.

The Tall Man.

I screamed.

My bedroom door flew open, banged against the wall.

Mommy stood in the doorway dressed in the pink, purple, and blue unicorn pajamas Daddy had helped me pick out for her on her birthday last month. Her dark, tangled hair hung down the sides of her face, clawed her shoulders with a million tiny fingers. She opened and closed her mouth, gurgling sounds dribbling out with the spit. They ran down her chin together, dripped on the floor at her bare feet. Her bright blue eyes were wide like saucers. They stared but didn't see anything. Red spots splattered her pajama top, smeared down one leg, soaking the cuff just above her foot.

She held Daddy's gun in her hand. It shook as she banged it against her leg.

"Mommy?" I said, my voice little and mouse-like. Not brave like I wanted it to be. "Where's Daddy?"

Her blank stare focused, turned toward me.

She hiccupped, wiping the spit from her chin with the hand holding the gun. "Why did you do it?"

The whispers grew louder, wilder. They pushed their way into my brain, where they danced and spun with sugar-fueled frenzy.

Pain throbbed behind my eyes. I pressed my hands against them, tried to push the thumping out of my head.

A name slid through the scraping noise. A face chased after it, followed by the monster with the stick-thin face. The Tall Man. "Dulcinea."

"No!"

I opened my eyes.

Mommy stepped through the doorway into my bedroom, tapping the gun against her waist. Anger twisted her face, burned behind her eyes.

She waved the gun at me, shiny and silver, glinting in the desperate light crouching in my room.

"Why?" she asked again. "Why did you do it? Why couldn't you just leave it alone?"

Red goo sagged from the hem of her pajama top, splatted onto the floor at her feet.

I shook, my knees pulled to my chest, my hands trying to keep them from banging into each other. I opened my mouth; the lie waiting for me to let it out where it could spin its web. She slid a wet, red-smeared envelope from her pajamas.

"Why?" Mommy screamed, shaking the envelope I'd taken from her secret hiding place at me.

The lie died.

"I...I put it back where you had it," I said. "I didn't know you didn't want Daddy to see what was inside. I—"

My voice crept back into my throat like a whipped dog. Mommy held the whip. "Daddy saw me put it back. He wanted to see what was in it. I didn't know you didn't want him to see the pictures. I swear!"

She laughed, the sound like scraping fingernails across a chalkboard.

"Stupid, stupid girl," she said. Her voice shook. "If you only knew what you've done."

"But—"

"No," she said. "It's too late for 'buts.' I told you to stay out of my things. Why couldn't you just listen to me for once, instead of being a little witch!" She sucked in a hissing breath, blew it out in a thunderstorm of contempt and rage. "Daddy's little girl," she said, slapping the side of her head with the gun. She giggled, the sound snotty-thin and runny, her lips pulled back in a smile that didn't reach her eyes. "Why the hell couldn't you have been Mommy's little girl? Huh? Why!"

I shook my head, mouth trembling, eyes watering with crocodile tears that spilled down my cheeks and dripped from my chin.

"You ruined everything. Did you know that? And now Mommy has to punish you for your sin, like she punished Daddy for his."

She shoved tangled strands of hair from her face. An awful, angry bruise pulsed down the side of her head to the bottom of her chin. Black, blue and red twined together in a fuming braid that seethed with each trembling breath.

Hissing slid from the phone I'd dropped beside my dresser, chased by a small, faraway voice.

Mommy looked at the phone, at me. But it wasn't Mommy that looked at me. A whispered name. "Dulcinea." My stomach twisted.

She gripped the gun so tight her hand turned white. The blue in her eyes was dark and dead. She raised the gun, pointed it at me. "Who did you call?"

I tried to swallow, found only fear, dried and dead in the back of my throat. "I—" I said. Barely a whisper.

Mommy smiled a sad smile.

The shadow of the Tall Man rose behind her. A long arm reached down, grasped her hand with a bony hand, the fingers like clawed spider legs. The face leaned forward, over her shoulder, whispered into her ear. The pale, colorless lips kissed the nape of her neck.

The red, glowing eyes turned to me. I wanted to be afraid of him, but I couldn't. Longing filled me. I reached toward him, my fear forgotten.

Mommy touched the gun to the side of her head, pulled the trigger.

A deafening boom stuffed cotton into my ears, yanked an earsplitting ringing from my head. I smashed my hands against the sides of my head. I shrieked, the sounds torn from my chest, my throat raw and shredded.

Mommy's head jerked to the side, the gun falling from her hand. The Tall Man lowered her to the floor and stepped over her body. He hugged a book to his chest, the charcoal black cover tattered, its edges frayed and singed, his red eyes glowing, dripping fire down his dead man's face into his horse-tail mustaches and scraggly beard.

He stood over me, opened the book, his twiggy lips stretched thin like a rubber band. "Dulcinea," he whispered as he lowered the book toward me, the pages fluttering feather-light in the breeze of his breath. "Welcome to our story."

My whole body throbbed. A hand squeezed my chest, leaving me dizzy and gasping. Fire raged behind my eyes, like when I stared too long into the sunset. I leaned forward, my mouth falling open as I rose to meet the pages and the words spilling out from them. I reached for them, fingers touching the scratchy surface.

Lightning grew behind my eyes.

I stepped from my body; sank into the story he held out to me. The covers closed, my body sagging to the floor. Bliss surrounded me, pushed away the fear and the terror, like when Daddy hugged me before tucking me into bed.

"No!"

The abrupt shout, like the head of a hammer, tapped the crystal bottling me. It shattered. I cried out, stumbled back against the wall, sank to the floor, sobbing, hands pressed into my face, trying to push the lightning splinters from my eyes.

Mommy's friend, the man hugging and kissing her in the pictures, gripped the Tall Man by his shoulders and wrenched him away from me, stepped between us, hands clenched at his sides, shoulders heaving, breath wheezing into the volcanic silence shaking the room.

"She's mine!" Mommy's friend said. "You can't have her. I won't let you take her."

The Tall Man leered, a willowy finger stabbing the air between us. "Ah," he said, flashing eyes burning with a fire that seared my heart with longing. "Such devotion. Such love." The dead smile grew, turned the corners of slitted lips upward toward the fiery eyes. "I, too, knew such love and devotion." He gestured toward my mommy. "As did she." The smile melted away, left behind flaming wrath. "Join Sophie. Together, you may find redemption for your sins."

The man standing between us faltered, stumbled a step forward, and sank to his knees, his trembling hand reaching for the gun that lay beside my mommy.

The Tall Man's gaze lit, the fire renewed and burning brightly, and scoured away the worming doubt.

Sirens shattered the silence. Red and blue flashing lights followed. Cars screamed into our driveway, screeched to a stop, sliding through ice and frozen snow. Metal doors slammed. Men shouted. Footsteps clattered up onto the new wooden deck Daddy had built last summer. The front door banged open.

I fell back into my wilting body. I sobbed, the sound bursting into the air like fireworks. My chest heaved. I gasped, a new and terrible pain pounding the inside of my head.

Longing.

A crumpled page, the gilt edges dulled, the ink faded, one side ragged and torn, fell to the floor at my feet, smoldering, tendrils of stinking smoke trailing into the air.

The Tall Man stepped back, scowling, his face etched with dismay and stunted desire, the book in his skeleton hands throbbing. His warm, welcoming smile melted from his twiggy lips, replaced by a seething yearning that ripped my heart in two.

He slammed the covers closed, tucked the book into his soot-grimed coat.

I blinked.

He cast a last longing glance at me, snarled at my mommy's friend slumped on his knees between us, and turned and strode from my room, the swirling touch of ash and charred wood brushing my nose and tongue.

I snatched the page from the floor, crawled after him, bawling, hunger ripping my heart from my chest. "Don't go!" I pleaded. "I'm sorry. I'll be good. Please!"

A firm hand gripped my arm, yanked me into a crushing embrace.

The light snuffed out, plunged me into an empty darkness. My heart ached. I cried out, hunger clawing past my desire. I squirmed in the man's grasp as he held me tight against his chest. "Let me go!"

"No," the voice a hoarse whisper, dripping regret and grief. "I won't lose you both."

I thrashed against him a moment longer, settled as the light found its way back. Clutching the torn page to my chest, I stared into my mommy's dead eyes, their empty glare stabbing me with blame and reproach.

Sam Pellerman

Blue and red flashing lights ricocheted off the ragged line of blue spruce, ponderosa pine, and corkbark fir guarding the Daugherty estate, the tips of the trees swaying hypnotically in the muttering wind. A stringy, cotton candy snow drifted from the night sky, dusting the ice-packed gravel driveway.

The sprawling two-story ranch house brooded in the snow-bright shadows, the granite and cedar board and batten walls scowling from the gloom. Mud-stained snow trampled the steps to the covered wrap-around red wood deck hugging the house. Snow glinted on the pine-green corrugated metal roof.

Viridescent light crept through gauzy curtains draped across frost-tinted glass, painting the deck with a ghostly green pallor. Yellow-white light blazed from the second-story windows like lighthouse beacons.

Sam Pellerman, Chief of Police for Ruby Creek, Colorado, nudged his cruiser past the first police SUV, the all-weather tires crunching the compacted rock like crushed bone as he pulled beside a second unit. Two Ruby Creek Memorial Hospital ambulances squeezed between the two police SUVs, their backs facing the front porch, doors flung open.

Two of Sam's volunteer officers stood at the bottom of the muddied stoop, hands shoved deep into their coat pockets, shoulders hunched, their stoic expressions pasty and faded in the glare of his headlights. Steamy clouds boiled from their noses and mouths before evaporating into the deeper nighttime darkness.

Sam stared, gripping the steering wheel, thinking about the time he'd spent helping Jim Daugherty build that deck last summer.

He stopped beside the second SUV, his cruiser's brakes squealing in quiet protest. To his left lounged a sleek, powder-blue 1985 Chevy Blazer belonging to the Garfield County Medical Examiner, Gale Henderson, Jim's best friend since grade school. He'd been Sam's best friend as well. Before Daisy came between the three of them and Deacon Barrett, their fourth wheel and Ruby Creek's ne'er-do-well heir and favorite prodigal son.

Sam swore under his breath, chewed his lower lip as he swung his gaze from Henderson's classic Blazer to the cryptic scene glaring down at him from the deck, his stomach gone sour, the bitter and burning taste of bile coating the back of his throat.

He reached for a cigarette, hesitated, an image of Daisy's disapproving glare burning a hole through the back of his skull.

He grimaced, crushed the cigarette as he rolled down his window to dump the crumpled tobacco and paper into the snow-littered night. The frost-bitten wind stammered through the opening, buffeted his face. Hushed voices rode the bitter cold air.

A shadow hunched at the edge of the deck, knees jammed against a broad, square chest, face sunk into quivering hands, sandy brown hair disheveled and wind-blown. Darkened stains streaked the jacket sleeves, the jeans, and the high-end boots jammed onto the top step.

Sam couldn't see them in the darkness, but he knew the boards surrounding the crumpled form were littered with snuffed cigarette butts.

Deacon Barrett.

"Damn it," Sam muttered as he shoved a piece of pink, granite-hard Bazooka bubblegum into his mouth, clamped his jaw closed as he unfolded himself from the car and slammed the door shut, the snowy fog tickling the ends of the hairs peeking out from beneath his hat. He met the nearest of his officers, Paul Rivers, at the bottom of the steps, yanked him close, their frosted breath entwining in an anxious dance.

"What the hell is he doing here?" Sam whispered through gritted teeth, his voice laced with venom.

Rivers winced, glanced over his shoulder at the huddled body crunched down at the top of the steps. "Sorry, Skipper," he said. "Deac was on scene when we arrived, just like that. Wouldn't move. Wouldn't respond. Just kept muttering, 'It's all my fault.' Over and over again." He cleared his throat. "He slugged Jake when he tried to pull him off the steps. That's when we found this." He held up an evidence bag containing a blood-smeared silver snub-nosed revolver.

Sam blew out a breath, ground the bubblegum between his teeth, and took the evidence bag, shifting it in his gloved hands. He squinted through the murky, snow-laced night at the glinting surface, looked up at Deacon. "Did he—"

"No," Rivers said. "He didn't even acknowledge it. Just stood at the top of the steps while we collected it, then sat back down, like he is now." He looked down at his shoes. "Thought we'd wait for you."

The bile in the pit of Sam's stomach burned to ash. "Inside?"

The color drained from Rivers' face. He shoved his hands into his pockets, pulled them out, crossed his arms, dropped them to his sides. "Bad." He shook his head, ran a quivering hand through his hair, shoved his cap back down over the top of his head, blinking melting snow from his eyes. "Jim and Sophie. Blood. Everywhere. And worse. Never seen anything like it. Don't want to see anything like it again."

An image rose in the back of Sam's mind, churned his stomach into a scalding stew.

"Emmie?" he asked, his voice weak, threatening to drop him like a rock into the abyss.

Hesitation.

"Unharmed. Whole. As far as we can tell. Splattered with blood. And worse. None of it hers. Scared as hell." He paused, pinched his lips together. "Keeps asking for her daddy."

Sam stepped toward the deck.

"The deputy mayor is inside," Rivers said. "She's with Emmie."

This just gets better and better.

Sam vaulted up the steps, stopped beside Deacon for a breath, hands clenching and unclenching, left it alone until he knew more. And that Emmie was okay. He turned back to Rivers. "If he so much as twitches, shoot him."

He stopped two steps inside the yawning threshold, gum popping into the sudden nervous silence. A garish light battered the front room, scrubbing the hues from the soft browns and sandstone pinks littering the open spaces, sanding the flesh from the bones underneath.

Restless shadows glared down from the vaulted, spruce-beamed ceiling, clawing at the islands of rustic, wildlife-themed throw rugs dotting the living room floor. A sandstone fireplace stood against the far wall. Smoldering coals glowed from inside its murky maw. Pine-scented candles, faux pine branches, and recent family photos adorned the teak mantel.

Sam's gaze roamed the taupe walls, searching for darker splotches and smears.

The tentative scents of orange, jasmine, and rose, a perfume Sophie favored, floated through the room, mixing with the stench of carnage wafting down the stairs from the second floor, and chased by the strained, haunting echoes of whispered voices.

Jim and Sophie's six-year-old daughter, Emerson, hunkered back into the depths of an over-stuffed pastel blue fabric recliner, the cushion seams and arms smeared with darker smudges and spots. She hugged her knees to her chest, pajama pants crusted with blood, orange-blossom hair hanging lifelessly over her hunched shoulders, clover-green eyes glistening with terrified tears.

Bethany Hunt, the Deputy Mayor of Ruby Creek, dressed in a rumpled, over-sized men's beige and brown plaid flannel shirt, wrinkled, distressed jeans, and shearling wool-lined snow boots, knelt beside the chair, clasping Emerson's tiny hand in her own. Her signature black Canada Goose Alliston winter coat lay sprawled on the floor behind her, a pair of tan, doe skin gloves peeking out from the pockets. She'd pulled back her tousled ash-blonde hair into a high ponytail, shaving ten years off the thirty-five she confessed to have lived.

Hunt looked up when Sam strode through the open doorway. Her fashion model complexion faded to a bloodless white, expression blank, dark eyes sunken into her sharply angled face, narrow lips quivering. A tainted angel struggling to maintain her faith.

And failing.

She snailed to her feet.

"Emmie?" Sam said.

Emerson glanced up, gasped. "Uncle Sam!" She poured herself from the chair, sprinted to him before Hunt could react.

Sam knelt and absorbed the full brunt of Emerson's weight. He scooped her up, grunted as she wrapped skinny, trembling arms around his neck, clutched his hips with her slender legs. He stood, bear-hugged her, her face buried in his shoulder, body shuddering with sobs, wetting his shirt collar.

Foreboding knotted his thoughts into an unruly tangle that strangled his breath.

Hunt skewered him with a questioning look.

Sam shook his head, mouthed, "Not now."

She hesitated, indecision warring across her burned-out expression. She slid back behind the chair, used it to support her fatigued weight, continued her wary watchfulness.

"I want my daddy."

Sam hushed Emerson, stroked her back with a gentle hand, allowed her to quiver against him, the tears crawling down his shirt. He hesitated. "I know, baby girl," he said. "I want your...daddy, too." He paused, swallowed back his own trembling sob and buried the grief as deep and as far as he could make it go.

Emerson hiccupped, pulled back from his shoulder, her eyes red and swollen, snot dribbling from her nose. She wiped it with the back of her pajama sleeve, blinked away the tears clinging to the corners of her eyes. Lifting herself in his arms, she craned her neck to look over his shoulder. "Where's mommy's friend?" she asked, her voice laced with trepidation.

Sam frowned, lowered Emerson to the floor, tried to crowbar her from his body. She refused to let go, continued to cling to him with octopus arms. He gave up, pulled her into another tight hug.

"What friend?" he asked.

"Mommy's friend," she said. "The man always with her in the pictures she kept in her secret place in the dresser. I found them and showed them to Daddy. He got really mad when he saw them. That's when Mommy came home, and they started yelling at each other and Mommy sent me to my room."

Sam frowned, loosened her grip enough to stare into her red, splotchy face, her eyes glimmering with new tears. A leaden weight sat in the bottom of his gut, tugging at the dread beginning to bubble in his chest.

"He saved me from the Tall Man and his book. Before your policemen got here."

Dread twisted Sam's gut. A fractured puzzle-piece picture formed.

The raspy voice slithered through his mind, tugging behind it the image of a tall, cadaverous figure, hidden by shadow, glowing red eyes, drooping mustaches caressing wiry, bloodless lips, skeletal hands sprouting spider-leg fingers that gripped a leather-bound book, the gilt edges singed with charcoal, the pages brown and yellowed with age, dark, caliginous ink smeared, the words unfocused and illegible.

The ravenous, rage-laced leer that wrung his soul and squeezed the life from his body.

The breathless whisper of a name. "Dulcinea."

The memory of his baby sister slumped over the edge of her bed, her dusty blue eyes dead and blank, cherub face gaunt and shriveled.

Sam shivered, licked drought-dry lips.

"His book?" Despite the terror strangling him, Sam reached for another memory, snagged the tattered edges before they dissolved.

Emerson dug a hand into her pajama pants, dragged out a crumpled, torn and threadbare page ripped from a book, the once scrubbed white surface stained yellow and brown by time.

Sam took it, held it to the light, squinting. The murky outline of a young child's face hovered at the edges of his perception. He turned the paper, gasped as the silhouette grew sharp and focused, his ripening dread driving glowing red spikes through his thoughts.

Sam shoved the page into his jacket pocket, stomped down the foreboding writhing in the pit of his soul. He crushed Emerson to him, squeezed until she wriggled in his grasp. A slow, burning resolve ignited in the core of his soul. *Not you, baby girl. If it's the last thing I do in this life, not you.*

"The Tall Man can't hurt you now," he said, his voice quaking.

She hugged his neck. "I want to thank Mommy's friend for saving me."

A new lump knotted Sam's gut. He screwed his eyes closed, asked, knowing and dreading the answer that would sprout from Emerson's lips. "Where is your mommy's friend now?"

"Outside."

Sam resisted the urge to strangle and shoot Deacon himself.

He knelt, pried Emerson from his chest. "Baby girl," he said. "I have to do my job now." He nodded toward Hunt. "I need you to go with Ms. Hunt and stay with her until I'm done."

Emerson squealed, clutched his neck. "Don't make me go," she cried. "I want to stay with you until I can see my daddy and mommy again." She pressed quivering lips to his ear. "I don't want the Tall Man to get me."

Sam unhooked Emerson's arms from his neck, handed her to Hunt. Emerson struggled, writhed and wriggled, crying, tears flooding down her face.

"Don't make me go," she bawled. "I don't want to go. I want to stay with you!"

"And you will," Sam said, his tone calm. He took Emerson's face between his hands, kissed her forehead, smeared her broiling tears. "Ms. Hunt is going to take you to my house and stay with you until I'm done here. She'll keep you safe until I get back. And the Tall Man won't be able to get you. Ever."

Emerson sucked back the tears, wiped the snot from her nose. She stared into Sam's eyes, nodded.

Sam sighed, touched a finger to her lips, steadied her quivering chin. He stood and spoke to Hunt. "Here are my house keys. Turn on all the lights. Keep her with you. And keep her in the dining room. At the table. It's the center of the house and she knows that table. It makes her feel safe. And under no circumstances, leave her by herself. For any reason. At any time. Understand?"

Hunt clutched Sam's keys, glanced down at Emerson. "I don't think—"

"I don't give a crap what you may or may not think," he said. "You're part of this now, whether you want to believe in the Quixote or not." He held her gaze, waited for understanding to sprout from the roots of logic and disbelief, blossom, and ripen. "If you wanted to stay safe, you shouldn't have gotten involved with Jim."

"But we didn't—"

"Doesn't matter," he said. "It's what Sophie believed." He leaned in, whispered. "You unlocked the door. Allowed Jim and Sophie to open it. But you're the one that invited the ghoul in." He stepped back. "And now you're going to guard it until I get this shit sorted out and get back to the house. Understand?"

"And Gale? He isn't going to like this. She's covered in...evidence."

"I'll handle Gale."

She met his gaze, calculation glinting in her eyes. A tense few seconds clicked away.

"And Daisy?"

Sam ran a hand through his hair. "Out of town and on the road. Gives me a couple days to sort some of this out."

"And what about him?" She looked past Sam through the open doorway and into the dark at the shadowed form huddled into itself at the edge of the deck.

"Take Emmie out through the garage. I'll let Jake know."

Hesitation married to uncertainty.

"I'm sorry."

Sam snorted. "Confess it to your priest." He grabbed her arm. "Keep Emmie safe."

She knelt beside Emerson. "Come on, sweetheart," she said. "Let's get your coat so we can go to your Uncle Sam's house where we can keep you safe, and maybe a little warmer."

Emerson cast an uncertain look at Sam. He smiled back and nodded. "I'll be there as soon as I can."

With an unsettled expression haunting her face, Emerson sucked in a breath and allowed Bethany Hunt to dress her before leading her toward the garage.

Sam watched them disappear, churning with trepidation and indecision. He stared at Deacon Barrett's hunched back. He knew what needed to be done to clean this mess up, the sacrifices that were required. And the burnt offerings to be made to ensure Emmie's safety for now.

He didn't have to like it. He just had to do it. The Queen's expendable Executioner. The King was dead. Long live the Queen.

He clicked the mike on his shoulder radio. "Gillespie."

"Yeah, boss."

"Got a package coming your way from the garage. Stay with it. Make sure it gets delivered."

Static crackled for a moment.

"Copy that. Out."

Sam strode through the front door, stood behind Deacon. Crystalline flakes swirled across the boards, tapped the edges of his boots. The clammy hands of the brittle wind fingered his hair, ruffled his collar, slid cold-hearted and soulless down his back.

He shivered, hunched his shoulders, and rested his hand on the butt of his service pistol.

"Stand up," he said.

The twitch of a head in response. Deacon lifted his head, straightened, hands squeezing his knees. "And if I don't?"

Sam drew his weapon, touched it to the back of Deacon's head. "I'll put a bullet through that cesspool you call a brain and call it a day. It's what everyone who is anyone wants me to do. And it'll save my ass from the reaper. Unless you want to do the right thing and pay his price."

A throaty, humorless chuckle. "Where's my daughter?"

The confession no one wanted to hear and chose to ignore.

Two adult bodies scurried from the garage across the drive, a small, bundled body clutched between them. A car door opened, slammed closed. An engine roared to life. Tires crunched through gravel and ice.

"Not here."

Deacon shook his head. "You don't understand," he said. "You never did. No one did."

Sam pursed his lips. His hands shook. "I understand enough," he said. "I know you messed up. That you allowed this to happen on your watch."

Deacon looked over his shoulder. "Really?" he said. "You're going to drag us down that rabbit hole? She's alive, isn't she? I saved her, didn't I?"

"Did you?"

Deacon snorted, buried his face in his knees.

"And what about Sophie?" Sam asked. "You did one hell of a job saving her, didn't you?"

"Jim Daugherty never loved her," Deacon said. "Not really. Not in that way. And Sophie deserved better."

"So, what; you thought you'd be that 'better' for her?" Sam knelt behind him. "What made you think you could do the dirty on the down-low with the mayor's wife and no one would find out?"

A hushed sob.

Sam scowled. "You don't deserve Emmie."

"Neither did Jim Daugherty."

"More so than you."

Deacon sneered. "So intones the mighty and virtuous Samuel Pellerman, Knight Protector of the realm, keeper of the peace, and dispenser of everything upright, moral, and honorable." He looked up. "Thinks he's flighting the giants but is just tilting at the windmills. He shook his head, "Sticks and stones, brother."

"You're an asshole."

"Better than a self-righteous prick."

"Get up," Sam said. "I won't tell you again."

"We going to do this here? In front of witnesses?"

"That's up to you," Sam said. "You're a dead man, either way." He grabbed Deacon's shirt collar. "You stole his prize. And you know what he'll do to you if you leave here alive. Your choice."

Deacon pushed himself to his feet, faced Sam. "Make it quick."

"Make it look good."

Deacon screamed, thrust his shoulder into Sam's chest, drove him into the wall. He grappled for Sam's gun, pressed it under his chin, and pulled the trigger.

The Quixote

Ruby Creek, Colorado—December 20, 2024

The lilting soprano timbre of Doris Day singing "Que Sera, Sera" crooned in my mind as I stepped from the bus and lit a Camel. The sudden flare of the burning match reflected off dusty patches of white, flaky snow tossed down from dark, ragged clouds skidding through the sky.

I moved aside to allow three other passengers to disembark, flashing a debonair smile into the disapproving glare of an aged dame bundled in a false mink coat and faux cherry-red alpaca wool scarf.

She balked and stalked off, her stumpy black satin heels teetering through the slush. Her perfume lingered, the sour, rosy scent competing with the diesel stench belching from the back of the bus.

I pulled a slow drag, allowing the acrid sting to scrape across my throat before blowing a blue-white cloud into the frosted night air. I watched the old woman navigate the icy terrain, my thoughts lingering on her long and ignoble life, the goblets of anger and prejudice she guzzled from, the dregs spilling out, poisoning all that she touched.

My book rustled inside my coat, pages fluttering. "She is not for us," the parchment breathed.

She stumbled through a patch of brown snow, one foot skimming out from under her. A hushed expletive burst out and floated for an instant before evaporating into the misty air. She reclaimed her balance and stiffened as she thrust a secretive glare over her shoulder.

I smiled back.

Her gaze drizzling ire, she hitched the fake fur coat higher on her shoulders and continued her treacherous trek across the parking lot.

The deep-throated rumble of the idling diesel vibrated the asphalt beneath my feet, stroking my troubled thoughts with a calming hand as the few remaining passengers disembarked. I scrutinized each, meeting their quick, secretive glances and longer, more meaningful glares.

The last to tumble from the bus was a small family—husband, wife, and young daughter, perhaps six or seven, who sported raven black hair twisted into twin tails. Her wide-eyed, innocent expression stirred echoes of a long-cherished memory of another distant soul.

She gawked up at me as they passed, smiled shyly, and dropped her gaze quickly. But not before I met her with my own, warm and inviting. Her mother snagged her hand, pulling her away from my small universe. I tipped my hat when she glanced back my way, her eyes dark and wary, dripping a deer-like anxiety and caution.

"What are you looking at?" the girl's father said.

"Excuse me?"

"You heard me."

The man, possibly a beefy hand taller than I, more muscular, a good seventy-five pounds heavier, glared at me. He reeked of rage and violence. His breath, stinking of noxious spirits, blew stiff white clouds through the air between us.

I met his gaze, my expression cloaked, my hands firmly secured within the pockets of my leather winter duster. I clasped the cigarette between my lips, allowed the trailing smoke to waft lazily into the air. Pulling one last slow drag, the end burning a bright, murderous orange, I dropped the butt, smearing it into the slushy pavement beneath my boot.

"Merely a pleasantry," I said. "A warm smile and kind look for a young girl and her mother, traveling beneath the veil of a hard winter's eve."

His eyes narrowed. "Stay away from them. Us."

"Certainly."

The book sighed, tickled the immortal desire simmering within the core of my need. The long-lived recitation of names seared into the bowels of remembrance, dribbled from my lips. "Daugherty. McMillan. Pellerman. Barrett."

A pause.

Barrett.

This man, a tangled and diseased branch, rotting from the trunk. A suitable beginning to feed my justice.

I quelled the shudder rifling my body and smiled, the corners of my mouth falling short of my eyes.

He turned, stalked after his wife and daughter, barked at them to wait. They stuttered to a reluctant stop, shivering in the late evening chill. He grabbed the woman's arm and yanked her after him, the girl's hand clasped in her own, dragging her behind.

The bus driver exited, stood at the bottom of the steps and lit up, the orange-red glow illuminating his round face. He nodded toward me. "Better get your business done while you can," he said. "We'll be leaving sooner than you may want."

I chuckled at his inadvertent private joke. "How long before we reach Ruby Creek?"

He scratched the side of his head, tapped the ash from the end of his cigarette. "About two, three hours." He peered into the sky, blinking through the dusting of snow. "Maybe longer, in this weather," he said.

"But there isn't a regular depot in Ruby Creek." He puffed smoke between us. "Not many people stop there. Too small."

"I see."

"But I can let you off if that's what you want."

"Thank you," I said. "That would be most appreciated." Without waiting for his reply, I strode across the parking lot toward the visitor center, my urge blazing in the pit of my soul, burning sun-bright and hot.

The woman and her daughter huddled together unnoticed on a bench away from the small tornado of milling passengers that crowded around the vending machines. I studied them, how the girl leaned from her mother, how she kept her hands clasped in her lap despite an offer to take her hand.

The memory of another young girl from a nearly forgotten time stirred again, swirled ashes from the shadows into the dim light of yearning. I tasted her scent, touched her tender soul.

I started, found that I had closed my eyes, caught once more in the infinite circle of grief for that first soul lost lifetimes ago, ruined utterly by barbaric, heartless, and selfish men.

I smiled joylessly. Nothing had changed during the century of my burden.

The woman fidgeted, compulsively glanced at the lavatory entrances, at her own hands, and back. She chewed her lower lip, wiped her nose with the back of her wrist. Dark circles hung from her haunted eyes. A faded bruise slid out from behind the darkened lens of a pair of over-sized sunglasses, yellowing her cheek and jaw.

The wind caught a door, slammed it closed. The woman jumped and gripped the edge of the bench with white-knuckled fists, a crumpled tissue trampled underfoot. The girl scooted away from her, head lowered, chin tucked into her opposite shoulder, eyes squeezed closed.

My justice cried out for the girl, her fading innocence, slowly and quietly choked to death between the unyielding grip of an abusive father and a mother, who herself was abused.

I waited for the mob surrounding the vending machines to disperse, then purchased a soda, a bag of chips, and a candy bar. I dumped them into my coat pocket and slid into the men's privy, holding the door for an exiting line of three sheepish gentlemen.

A commode flushed, the sudden rushing waterfall echoing off grit-stained tiled walls. The metal door banged open. The unpleasant gentleman that had accosted me in the parking lot walked out. He smirked as he hitched and zipped his trousers. At the grimy sink, he stared at his reflection, running water into his cupped hands to splash across his face.

I locked the lavatory door and strode toward him, the quiet tapping of my boots echoing off the walls. Standing behind him, I doffed my leather fedora. "Excuse me, kind sir."

He glanced at me from the mirror, blinking water from his eyes. His loutish face twisted into an impatient scowl. "Didn't I tell you to leave my family the hell alone?"

I smiled. "Of course." I turned and paused, lifted a finger in sudden, feigned recognition, my disarming smile cold and calculating. "I believe I recognize you now," I said. "Bobby Barrett. Correct? Are you not a great grandson of Winston Barrett?"

He knitted his brows in confusion.

"What's it to—?"

I slammed his face into the mirror.

Glass cracked and splintered, sliced a gash across his forehead, smearing crimson across the fractures.

I drew his head back by the hair, bashed his face into the mirror once more, twitched a grim smile at the sound of crunching bone and cartilage.

I released him.

He staggered back, knees wobbly, face bludgeoned and bloody, his nose bent and crumpled to the side, dripping scarlet goo.

As he collapsed, I grabbed him by the back of his coat collar, staggered him into a nearby privy stall, hauled him onto the seat of a feces-smeared commode.

His head lolled to the side, eyes unfocused. I backhanded him, grasped his chin to ensure he could look me in the eye.

"Sir," I said, my tone gentle and even. "The woman traveling with you, who hides in the shadows for fear of the pain you inflict upon her, was a delicate flower once, which you have spoiled and trampled beneath the crushing weight of your boot." I paused, shifted my grasp to the front of his shirt, hauled him up like a sack of potatoes. "And the girl—" I shook, my fist twisting his shirt, winding his collar like a spring. He struggled feebly, choked, his gasping breath mingling with the red, tarnishing the blue and white tartan tweed.

"Ah, the girl." I threw him back down onto the commode. Porcelain crunched. "A life and spirit never given its god-graced opportunity to blossom or flourish. It is both a burden and a pleasure I take in freeing her from your strangling grasp."

I stood over him, rage burning hot and bright in my chest. He stared up at me, blood running down his forehead into his eyes. He wiped them clear, spat at me.

"Go to hell."

I pulled the jackknife from my coat, the metallic click of the unfolding blade rolling through the stilted silence, and drove it through his chest. "I have already been," I said as I twisted the blade and shoved the tip upward into his throbbing heart. "Alas, it is not a place one would wish to tarry." I yanked the knife free, smeared the steel clean upon his trousers. "For you, however, I believe the innkeeper shall make an exception." I washed the blood from my hands, face, and beard, smeared the worst of the gore from my duster with a damp towel.

I slipped from the lavatory into the lobby. It stood solemn yet watchful as I walked to the woman and her daughter. She looked up and twitched a nervous smile. The girl avoided my gaze, arms crossed defensively.

"May I sit?"

The woman scanned the emptiness, her gaze lingering for a moment on the alcove to the lavatories.

"You look thirsty." I fished the soda can from my coat pocket, held it out to her. She reached out hesitantly and grasped the can. Our hands touched, the whispered justice upon my breath ruffling the edges of her hair, caressing her mind with words only she could hear.

She shuddered as I released the can, the haunted look in her eyes dimming, her will yielding to my own. I looked past her to the girl. She stared for a moment, glanced at her mother, confusion warring with the delicate prick of fear. I smiled, reached across the woman's lap, set the candy bar into her small, delicate hand. My fingers grazed hers as she wrapped her fist around the wrapper, the fear in her eyes melting.

I looked at the woman, took the soda from her and set it on the bench, touched the back of her hand to my lips.

She sighed, sudden contentment pushing out the wary trepidation. She stared into the distance, visions of happiness rolling through her thoughts.

"The man in the lavatory," I said. "Your husband?"

She nodded.

I laid a box cutter into her open palm, closed her fingers around the handle.

She turned, looked at me, glanced down at the razor blade in her fist.

"He bid me tell you to join him."

I stood, drew her after me, pressed gentle lips to her cheek. "He is alone in the lavatory," I said. "And I shall guard the door as your faithful servant to ensure you are not disturbed."

She hesitated, spared a glance at her daughter. I gently propelled her forward. "No need to worry for the girl," I said. "I shall protect her as if she were my own." I watched her stroll across the lobby, pause beneath the lavatory entrance. She turned, uncertainty touching her eyes. I nodded. She vanished, the faint click of the lavatory door closing behind her.

"Where did my mother go?"

"To join your father." I drew the book from my coat, opened it, the crinkled edges of the parchment tickling the air. "Shall I read you a story while we wait?"

The girl swallowed, her eyes round and shining with eagerness. She nodded.

I read; the words flowing between us, winding their earthy magic through her heart, her mind, her soul.

A half-page read. She touched my hand. "Can I become part of your story?"

"Why certainly, my small, delicate dove. It is why I have come."

She stared at the page, licked her lips as she reached over to brush the faded parchment with trembling fingers. "Will it hurt?"

"No," I said. "It will not hurt. I promise." I turned the pages until I came to a blank leaf, held it for her to see.

She nodded, stared into the yellowed oblivion, her eyes slowly draining of their light. Her image appeared on the paper below her fingers, growing slowly with life and vigor as her physical body wilted, its soul drained away.

Four heartbeats later, her body slumped back against the wall, mouth slack, eyes empty and dark, skin pallid and dried, cheeks sunken. I turned the book, gazed at the portrait etched into the vellum, and smiled at the light shining from the doe brown eyes staring back up at me, a rose-colored flush brushing the cheeks, a playful expression glinting from the face, the elfish mouth curled into a frolicsome grin that warmed my thoughts.

An invisible hand scrawled a name below the image. Gracie.

"Hello, Gracie," I said, stroking the rich raven black hair sketched into the surface of the folio. I kissed her likeness before closing the book and dropping it back into my coat.

Ignoring the sudden piercing scream from the lavatory, I rose and strode into the embrace of the startling cold.

A heavy, urgent snow pelted the slushed blacktop, staining the yellow-tinged night with a cleansing white. I paused at the bus doorway, offered my hand to a dame as she struggled to mount the first step. She frowned and glared at my hand for a moment before taking it. I hefted her up the stairs, relinquishing her to the center aisle.

Our driver leaned forward in his seat, peered past the flapping wipers as they flung snow and ice from the frosted glass. He looked at me, grasping the door control. "Anyone else coming behind you?"

"Only the dead and the damned."

Emerson Daugherty

My daughter Maggie and I stood in the bowels of the Ruby Creek Memorial Cemetery.

The pale, chill hand of winter wind danced calloused fingertips across the back of my neck. I shivered and hunched lower into my coat, hands stuffed deep into my pockets. In one pocket, I trapped my daughter's small hand inside my own. In the other, I clutched an old and scarred leather-bound journal, a legacy of slaughter and retribution penned by an ancestor, Tristan Daugherty, gifted to me by the man who raised me, Sam Pellerman. Stuffed inside lay a sheet of paper torn from an aged book, the blurred, unfinished outline of a six-year-old girl etched onto the antique parchment.

I was that girl.

And I had come back to Ruby Creek to erase that sketch and end the story it belonged to, begun one hundred thirty years ago.

Maggie shivered beside me, teeth chattering quietly in the brittle afternoon air. A ragged line of winter storm clouds scraped across the faded blue sky, driven by the fitful wind. Shadows skipped across ice-burned grass, tapping the frozen edges of old, dirty snow piled against the base of headstones chiseled from marble, granite, and sandstone.

I sniffed the air, caught the scent of new and old death clinging to the breeze.

Three rows to the south, four men lounged beside the frosted arm of a backhoe, its mud-stained claw resting in the shallow bowl of a new grave. Steam tendrils rose from the lumpy dirt piled beside the hole.

My hands curled into fists inside my coat pockets as old, blood-stained childhood memories crawled out from the sewers of forget-fulness.

"Dulcinea." A thin, scratchy voice that caressed time-faded mem-ories with an eager lover's trembling touch.

"Mommy, you're hurting my hand."

"What?" I glanced down at Maggie, wincing as the cringe twisted her round, rosy-cheeked face.

"Sorry, baby," I said, relaxing my fist as she tugged her hand from mine and pulled it from my pocket.

She held it to her chest, rubbing it. "I'm cold." She looked up at me. "When can we go back to the hotel?"

I graced her with a wan smile, knelt and took her hands in mine. "I know you're cold, baby. We're almost done, and then we can go back to the hotel and get warm."

"And swim in the pool?" Her eyes lit up, melting the chill in the air between us.

I huffed a chuckle, brushed her forehead with a fond kiss, and stood. She slid her hand into mine, leaned her head against my leg, her breath blowing miniature clouds into the grasping wind.

The sky spat sleety pebbles. The sun shivered, trapped behind a tattered curtain of stormy gray clouds, melting shadow and light to-gether.

Freeing myself from my daughter's grasp, I knelt, touched the frozen granite of my dad's headstone, ran trembling fingertips across the name and date etched into the stone. 'James Daugherty. Loving husband and father. Taken too soon.'

"Is that Grampa?"

I pinched a fleeting smile, wiped the tears from my cheeks. "It's Mommy's daddy," I said, looking down at her. "Mommy just wanted to say hi while we're here. We'll see your grampa tomorrow."

"When we say goodbye to the b—"

"Maggie!"

She froze, the unformed word stuck to her pink lips. She wiped her mouth with the back of her hand. "Sorry," she said.

I chuckled, hugged her. "It's okay, baby. Just don't use that word when we're with Grampa."

She nodded, her expression solemn. She stepped forward, placed her hand on the top of the headstone, her six-year-old fingers tickling the rough-hewn edges. "Do you think he knows we're here?"

She looked back at me.

I pulled her into my arms, set my chin on top of her head. "Yes," I said. "I think he does."

"Who's that?" She pointed at the grave next to my dad's. "Is that your mommy?"

A sudden chill danced down my back. The sleet drizzled in ragged sheets from the churning sky. I was six again.

The Tall Man stood in my bedroom doorway, an eager need throbbing behind his eyes. My mom lay lifeless at his feet, eyes glowering with guilt and blame, blood soaking the ivory carpet, her gore-spattered hand clenching a revolver.

Spindle-shanked hands lovingly offered an open book to me, its gilt-edged pages curled and cracked, faded and stained a vomit yellow.

I stared into a blank page, its emptiness intoxicating, promising peace and a painless release.

The throaty, choking roar of a diesel engine. A metallic thunk.

I jumped, stumbled back onto my heels, my heart stuttering. My memories swirled, melted away into a gooey mess, sucked my mom and her accusing eyes through a narrow straw down into a gaping cavern.

The backhoe coughed to life, blew black smoke into the roiling sleet beginning to shower the cemetery.

I breathed. Maggie stared at me with super-sized eyes, uncertainty clutching her cherub face. She sat splayed over my mother's grave, dingy white pellets clinging to her hair. I looked past her at the headstone. A ghostly image hung suspended over her grave, the glowing eyes burning with breathless need. It evaporated an instant later, tattered edges stolen away by the jerking wind.

"You okay?"

My daughter screamed. I spun, reached clumsily into my jacket, searching for my pistol.

A man wearing wet, mud-stained coveralls, rubber snow boots, a tattered Colorado Rockies ball cap, and thick, leather work gloves staggered back, hands raised in surrender. He shook his head, flicking snow from the ragged bill. "Hey dude, calm down." He nodded past us. "We heard a scream, thought maybe someone needed some help. But if you—"

"Yeah, sorry," I said, smoothing water-logged hair behind an ear as I gathered my shattered wits and stood, brushing frozen dirt and snow from my pants. I grabbed Maggie's hand, scooped her into my arms. She buried her face in my chest, hugged my neck in a death grip. "The backhoe," I said. "It startled my daughter when you started it up."

He continued to stare for a moment longer than necessary, his jaw working, his eyes trying to decide if they believed me or not.

"Really. We're okay. It's just…loud noises scare her." I brushed past him, strode through the patchy ice toward the path that led back to my GMC, the weight of watching eyes tugging at the back of my jacket.

Sam Pellerman

Sam Pellerman huddled over his family dining room table, helter-skelter stacks of time-grimed file folders and coffee-stained papers littering the scarred and scuffed surface. Accumulated evidence from the past one hundred thirty years. Family murders and suicides; husbands and wives, fathers and mothers, young daughters. Troubled homes and relationships.

Always the descendants from the four Ruby Creek founding family lineages.

Daugherty. McMillan. Barrett. Pellerman.

Beads on a string, one torn off in each generation. Random. But always involving the same four families. Direct and indirect descendants. Jim and Sophie Daugherty. The final sacrifice from the previous generation. Emerson. The last payment, but uncollected because of Deacon Barrett's interference, for which he'd paid the ultimate price.

Sam grimaced, threw back the last of his bourbon, refilled the glass. He rifled through the copied pages from Tristan Daugherty's personal journal. The man responsible for the Quixote.

Had Emerson found the original journal and her page from the Quixote's book he'd hidden in the sparse belongings she'd tossed into the back of her GMC the day she fled Ruby Creek? Had she read it? Would she believe any of it? Would she want to believe any of it?

Hope flapped broken wings before plummeting to the ground.

Beside the scattered stacks of papers lay three rows of photographs. Jim Daugherty smiled from the top row. Emerson from the middle. And at the bottom, Deacon Barrett. Always on the bottom, Deacon. Sam twitched a regretful smile at his unintended pun, guzzled his four-fingered glass of bourbon, slopped the last of the bottle into his glass while continuing to stare at the three rows of photos.

Twenty-year-old denial squatted beside him, the drunken memory of Deacon's suicide confession sloshing through his thoughts. His gaze flicked from Deacon to Emmie and back, photo to photo, age to age. He shook his head. How many times had he repeated this exercise? Hundreds? Thousands? Millions?

But no matter how adamantly he wanted to deny it, he always circled back to the same unwelcome conclusion. Deacon had told the truth about Emmie's parentage before they blew a hole through his brain. To dodge the Quixote's rebuke for denying him his prize.

He glowered at the photos, rage simmering, bubbling and spitting, bouncing the pot lid with each jarring burst.

Did Emerson know? Did it matter?

Not if she never came back to Ruby Creek.

But that didn't change the fact that Emerson was now the center of the Quixote's curse. The progeny of a Barrett. Claimed by a Daugherty. Raised by a Pellerman. Romantically connected to a McMillan. She'd become the linchpin holding the curse together.

Which meant what?

Sam paused, lifted his glass, peered through emptiness into an aberrant and misshapen world. When had he emptied his glass? He reached for the bottle, fingers fumbling the catch, watched with drunken fascination as it wobbled and fell over, and rolled off the table, crashing to the floor.

He slouched over the table, one hand clenching the empty whiskey glass, the other splayed across the chaos of photos scattered by his clumsiness. Deacon and Emmie smiled at him, their photos touching, father and daughter, their familial resemblance unmistakable.

Had the Quixote known?

If so, why hadn't he returned to claim his stolen prize?

He thought of the torn page bearing the indistinct image of a young girl Emmie had given him that night.

For a moment, Sam wished he'd kept it, hidden it. Or destroyed it. But would any of those actions have changed the course of history?

Twenty damned years and he still asked the same questions, still didn't have the answers.

And now, a new generation had risen, ripened, and was ready to be plucked.

Would the Quixote return to reap the new fruit from the Founding Trees? Or was he waiting for the prize denied him to return? Or both?

If their four families were the beads on the string, Ruby Creek was that string, the thing that tied them together.

Vigilance. Absence.

They were the only shields he had.

Keep Emmie away. Wait for the Quixote to appear. Destroy him and his book.

A perfect plan. Except for Daisy's death.

Despite his best efforts, Emmie would find out, and she'd come back. Not for Daisy, but for his sake.

Uncertainty crept into his thoughts. He glanced at his cell phone, the urge to call Emmie crawling through his mind, to tell her he didn't want or need her help.

Sam threw his glass. It shattered against the far wall, sprayed bour-bon-soaked shards across the floor. He shoved the scattered photos and unruly piles of papers away, calloused fingertips grazing the marred table surface.

Hackberry.

Hand carved and machined. Assembled under the strict and skilled supervision of his dad. A surprise wedding present for Daisy. One of a kind. Golden tan, irregularly striped, with darker brown arteries following the meandering path of the grain, mottled by flat, oval, charcoal-black knots.

He laid trembling hands on the burnished wood, his fingertips catching the lifetime of notches and nicks in the surface. Where Emerson, in a fit of defiance on her eighth birthday, had carved her name into the wood with a pocketknife she'd stolen from his tackle box. Later, his name had followed. And finally, reluctantly, *Daisy*, her resentful heartbreak softened for the moment by the fiery determination of a young girl desperate for the love of a mother to replace the one she lost.

Almost a family, after two long, heartrending years, battered and beaten by memories of death, destruction, and worse.

Their table. Their family. A delicate flower resurrected from the flames of despair and sorrow, loved and cherished the best he knew how, despite the ghostly specter looming ravenously over their shoulders.

At least in that moment.

Muted light peeked through the slats of half-open black oak shutters, sliced across well-traveled beige carpet, the sharp, blinding ends picking at the soles of Sam's discarded shoes. Dust motes danced through the light, glittering with broken promises and stabbing regrets.

Whetstone-sharpened memories of that night twenty years ago when their world fractured into a million pieces.

Sam heaved a sigh, lowered his head to the table, and wept.

An icy breath shivered through the warm air, pricking the ends of the hairs on the back of his arms. Wood floor planks creaked beside him.

He looked up, wiped the bitterness from his eyes.

"Hey, Sammy boy. How's the pain pounding the back of your skull?" A low, cynical chuckle. "Nothing to say?" A pause, the air hovering around the table shivering with anticipation. "You look like shit."

"Go away."

"You wound my heart, Sammy."

"You're dead, Barrett."

Quiet laughter grazed the back of Sam's neck.

"You sure about that?"

"We used my gun to kill you the night our world fell apart."

The chair beside him scraped against the floorboards.

"Noooo! And I thought I was just suffering from an eternal case of heart-stoppage. You sure?"

"I still feel your hand around mine when we pulled that damned trigger."

"Huh. Guess that explains why no one from the old gang ever visits. Except for maybe Jim. When they let him out of hell. But hey, we all can't be as popular as you, can we?"

Sam's breath frosted the air. He looked at the chair beside him. "What do you want?"

"Can't a friend just visit to pay his respects?"

"We weren't friends."

"Oh, hey, you still hanging onto that? Daisy chose you, didn't she? Used goods, though. Happens dude. Besides, Sophie was much better. Nothing better than popping that—"

"Shut the hell up." Sam slammed his palms down.

The air grew thick and silent.

"Hey, want a beer? Or something stronger? Beer just doesn't cut it when you're mourning, does it?"

Sam blinked, didn't remember walking to the liquor cabinet. He stared through his transparent reflection in the cut glass at the chair squatting beside his, and the ghoulish outline lounging within its loose embrace. He tried to swallow past the lump clutching the back of his throat, images of the Alzheimer's that had chowed down on Daisy's brain dancing a macabre chorus line across his thoughts. Step. Step. High kick. Step. Step. No memories. Step. Step. Die.

Memories of her desperate, agonized cries at the end hunkered vulture-like at his shoulder.

"I killed you," he whispered as he leaned his forehead against the cabinet door.

Wood grated and scratched. Papers fluttered, skinned quiet paths over the tabletop.

"No worries. I can see you're not in the mood for company. Shit happens. And I gotta tell you, you're hip deep in the guano. You sure you don't want that drink? I don't think Daisy will mind. She's kinda busy at the moment, anyhoo. You know, servicing the guys."

The air shivered.

Sam threw a bottle of bourbon at the chair. It skipped off the tabletop, skittered across the floor and shattered against the wall.

"Get the hell out." Sam pressed his back against the liquor cabinet, his knees threatening to buckle. He swiped at the sweat pricking his forehead.

"She's back, you know. Came to help you bury the mindless corpse of your whore."

"Who's back?" Sam asked. But he knew the answer to his question. And dreaded it.

"Can we say her name, now that Daisy's feeding the worms? Or is Emerson still persona non grata?"

Silence, except for the scrape of Sam's breath across the stagnant air.

The shadows leered at him, crawled along his flesh, maggoty and rotted. Sam staggered toward the table, slapped his hand against the top to steady himself. "She can't be here," he said. "I didn't—"

"Oh, hey, we took care of that for you. Knew you were a little distracted. You're welcome."

Sam shook his head, panic winding its way up from his gut to strangle his heart. "I didn't want—"

"Why? Thought you'd like to have your pretend daughter back for the final nuptials. Now that the bitch is dead." An amused pause. "You know, that kinda has a nice rhyme to it. Like in the Wizard of Oz." Hushed humming filled the silence.

Sam sucked down a breath but couldn't make his lungs work. He gagged.

"Hey, big guy, settle down." A frigid breath stroked his back between his shoulder blades, making him shudder. "Maybe choke down a bottle of those little white pills Gale Henderson prescribed for you. Chase it back with the bottle of the really good stuff. That'll do the trick. Nice and neat. And painless. Well, kind of."

Sam collapsed to his knees, pounded the table with his hand. "No," he whispered, tears gathered at the corners of his eyes. He pulled himself to his feet, staggered to pick up the chair and slammed it into the floor. He stood over it, clenching and unclenching his fists.

"Tsk, tsk, old friend. Is that any way to treat your dear lamented whore's furniture?"

Silence wrapped rotting fingers around Sam's throat as he stared down at the splintered chair.

Sam wiped the snot from his nose, peered into the shadows crouching in the far corner of the dining room, blinked away the eyes staring out at him from the darkness. He staggered toward them.

"Get the hell out."

A low, feral chuckle answered his demand. "Before I go, old buddy, thought I'd bring you some good news."

A frosted breath of air whistled through the room.

Sam closed his eyes, shivered.

"This is going to be the big guy's last appearance. Don't want to miss the show."

Sam gaped, foreboding winding coils around his soul.

A leer pricked his heart.

"Don't worry, Emmie ain't the main course. She's too old. Too immoral. Too sinful. Too spoiled. Guess the shrinks were right. We think we're preparing them for the world. But what we're really doing is tenderizing them before shoving them into the oven. She's still a sweet dish, though. Big Guy is gonna have her for dessert."

Wood creaked.

"What he wants is that scrumptious bundle of joy Emmie pushed out from between her legs after our delectable Daisy tossed that little bird from the nest like so much garbage. You know, fresh meat. Wink. Wink."

Frigid breath battered Sam.

"The Big Guy thanks you for gifting Emmie's page back to her when she got the hell out of Dodge. Now that's she's back, it frees him to do his duty. Free and unencumbered, unfettered and unbound. You know, stuff like that. The old boy does wax poetic."

Sam shuddered, collapsed into his chair. The ghostly image of a six-year-old girl who looked like Emmie at that age with juniper-green eyes and curly dark auburn hair stared back at him, her tiny mouth puckered into the beginning of a delighted grin.

"You know, Sammy, you might want to sober up and get some rest. It's going to be a bumpy night." The wave of a ghostly hand in mock salute. "See you in hell, my friend."

The Quixote

I lounged on a raven black wrought-iron bench streaked with clown-nose red rust across the street from the Ruby Creek Elementary school, legs crossed, hands relaxed in my lap. Creedence Clearwater Revival's "Bad Moon Rising" soothed my thoughts, John Fogerty's earthy, gravel-laden voice pleasantly scraping away the detritus clinging to the frayed fringes of the hole that had once housed my soul.

The skeletons of slumbering quaking aspens stood behind me, barren branches trembling in the frigid air. The wind stood stagnant, the acrid stench of blood and rage squatting beside me.

The mid-morning sun hung from the top of a lusterless, cloudless blue sky, light fuzzed and frayed by the winter chill.

The scattered cries and raucous laughter of young children from the elementary schoolyard across the street danced enticingly beside the quiet, hushed tones of passing traffic two streets over.

Carrion crows stood guard from the branches overhead, calling the dead to the rollicking party.

I sighed, glanced skyward, release huddling just out of my reach. Had only another generation passed since I'd last set foot in Ruby Creek? It seemed a lifetime, at least. The innocent cried out to me, demanding that I slake their thirst for the justice I'd left pooling at my feet, my task unfinished, the soul of my greatest regret no longer innocent, but stained by the world's corruption.

Her unblemished and immaculate daughter was now the object of my desire.

She would become my last Dulcinea, her mother beside us. My beloved Nayara reborn. The final offerings to pay the penance for their grievous sins.

A breath of frosted air brushed my cheek. I thought to shiver at its touch, declined the invitation as a shadow settled onto the bench beside me, dimming the light, bringing to mind the memory of black, ash-laden smoke and the stench of burned flesh.

"Is the message delivered?" I asked.

The air beside me rippled, joined by a malevolent chuckle. "It was my pleasure."

"Sadism is a baser instinct. It does not become you."

"Oh, but it is so lip-smackingly delicious. You can taste the snap, crackle, and pop as you grind down the resolve and courage, mash it into a soupy mush before spoon-feeding it back."

I frowned. "Do not forget our gentlemen's agreement."

A hesitant silence. Followed closely by uncertainty, and perhaps regret.

"How could I ever forget such a sweet and succulent covenant and the promises given and agreed upon?

"For the sake of your tatterdemalion soul, pray that you do not." I paused, met his ire. The ice-hardened furor dulled, the flames banked. I smiled.

"He took my life from me," he said. "I thought I might return a portion of the favor."

"Your life was your own to do with as you wished."

Smoke rose from the acid burning through the icy air.

I turned, stared into the fire of raging hatred, unafraid. For I had created it. "Our choices," I said, "have consequences. Did you not stop to think that your choices would burn your world and the world of those around you to ash?"

"I would not have shot myself."

"Perhaps. Your guilt, however, could not be denied."

"You're the devil."

"I am justice," I corrected. "And you are its able servant, come to ensure that the innocent receive their due.

"The devil," he repeated.

I chuckled. "Believe what you will. As long as you accomplish the tasks I set before you."

"Pellerman is mine, as we agreed?"

"When the task is complete."

"And—"

"We have discussed this," I said. "The answer remains 'no.' Emerson Barrett Daugherty Pellerman McMillan and her daughter, Maggie, are my Nayara and Dulcinea. You assured their fate when you interfered in the Reaping a generation ago."

His rage boiled for a heartbeat.

"Decisions. Actions. Consequences. You cannot escape them."

The slow clutching crack of rubber strolling across asphalt, accompanied by the throaty grumble of a car motor, approached. Brakes squealed, dragging the vehicle to a stop in front of me. Exhaust boiled from the tailpipe, the hoarse rumble from the engine drowning out the sounds of childish laughter and playful screams from across the street.

Sancho slipped away, his passing a dirty iridescence, tarnishing the brisk early afternoon air.

I tipped my hat. "Constable."

"You're not from around here."

"I am not," I said. "Simply passing through your wonderful winter countryside. Thought I might stop and experience the quiet grandeur of your community for a few days."

"Uh, huh." He examined me for a breath, mistrust glinting from his dark, flint-hard eyes. "Where are you staying?"

I shrugged. "I have not yet decided upon a domicile. Do you have a suggestion? A local favorite, perhaps?"

"How long have you been sitting here?"

"I am not certain," I said. "Have I warranted such attention from the local constabulary?"

His gaze flicked to my coat pockets. "Mind if I see what you have in your pockets?"

"Not at all." I held out the sparse contents for his examination.

He continued to study me, the distrust in his eyes burning brighter. "We got a call," he said. "About a stranger matching your description watching the school for several hours."

"Is that a crime?"

He shook his head. "No, but a stranger watching elementary school children play raises suspicions. Suspicions we would rather send on their way before a crime is committed."

"Ah, I see. My apologies for the misunderstanding. I did not realize that lounging on a park bench and enjoying a brisk winter day was a dubious activity. To cause no further concern, I shall be on my way."

I stood, tipped my hat.

"I don't think so." The engine silenced its grumbling purr. The driver's door broke open, metal hinges groaning into the quiet. The officer stepped from his car, right hand resting cautiously upon the butt of his sidearm. "Maybe I do have a suggestion for a place for you to stay while we sort this out." He motioned toward his vehicle, opened the back door. "If you wouldn't mind."

My book shivered with unexpected anticipation. The memory of the bus ride into Ruby Creek blossomed. My liberation of Dulcinea's trapped soul from its torment and fear.

Daugherty. McMillan. Pellerman. Barrett.

In one hundred thirty years, justice had never tasted so sweet. And...I rejoiced.

I flashed him a thin smile. "Are you not the great grandson of Orville and Rachel McMillan?" I asked. "You have children, do you not?"

"What?"

"You do, I believe. Two. Ages fifteen and ten. A boy and a girl."

He unsnapped the safety strap on his holster. "What the hell—"

"Your son is already sullied," I said. "Impure, his soul beyond redemption, corrupted by the world. Mostly yours. Pornography has no redeeming value and delights in destroying relationships and lives. And then there are the illegal substances he uses to poison his mind and body." I paused, pinned him with an accusatory stare. "Did you know he offered his ten-year-old sister to his friends as payment for the drugs?"

He gaped, anger flashing bright and deadly through the confusion drenching his eyes.

I sighed, my regret pushing him back a step. "Your son's perversions outshine even your own." I shook my head. "It is too late for him. I cannot save him. Nor would I wish to. But your daughter...an innocence still smolders deep within the core of her soul. If I reach her soon enough, I might still fan that fading coal into a flame again. But only if you are willing."

He drew his weapon. "On your knees, hands behind your head, fingers laced," he said, his tone edged with burning iron.

"Do you know where your wife, Linda, is at this very moment?"

He hesitated, the unwelcome truth flashing through his eyes, what he already knew but had been unwilling to admit. He lowered his weapon.

I stepped up to him, placed my hand on his shoulder. His eyes grew dim and empty. "I wish I could tell you that you are innocent of your wife's affair. But alas, I cannot. You wear your offenses around your neck as a millstone. It weighs you down, demands that I release you from your regret and guilt, and the ill choices you have made that drove your wife to seek the attentions of another man." I nodded toward the schoolyard. "Your daughter's homeroom teacher, in fact. Ironic. And tragic."

I slid the blade of my jackknife through his side, below the bottom edge of his flack-jacket and up under his ribs. He gasped, sagged against me as I twisted the knife. He dropped his gun. It clattered against the ice-littered concrete. The crows bearing witness took sudden flight, cawing into the stagnant morning air.

As the light died from his eyes and he sucked in a last, rattling breath, I leaned in, supporting his weight, guiding it into the backseat of his car. "The only solace I can offer in your last moment is that your wife and the man she is with shall both know justice as well." I paused, slicked a few errant strands of sweat streaked hair back from his forehead. "I will do what I can for your daughter. She at least deserves peace and safety. Your son, unfortunately, is beyond saving. He shall join you and your wife shortly."

His eyes widened. His lips moved.

I silenced him with a finger. "Do not speak. Your end has come, and you cannot alter your fate or that of your family."

One last shuddering breath shook his body.

I laid him across the back seat, quietly closed the door. I retrieved his sidearm, slid into the driver's seat, and placed it reverently beside me. A curious weapon, what they called a semi-automatic. I preferred revolvers. They were more elegant. But this would work for what I intended.

I started the engine, stared a moment at the wild crowds of children storming across the snowy field, their innocence uninterrupted and non-corrupted. I tipped my hat in silent and anonymous appreciation, shifted the car into gear and drove away, the wind kissing my face and tugging the sleeve cuff of my winter duster with eager anticipation.

Emerson Daugherty

Late morning scattered sunlight slanted through the hotel lobby windows. Discordant conversations buzzed, wasp-like, through the crowded breakfast area, punctuated by the mind-piercing cries of infants and toddler tantrums. Luke-warm manufactured air hummed behind the walls, heaved laborious breaths into the overhead open spaces and between the tables.

The lobby TV spouted a weather forecast about a snowpocalypse that could bury Ruby Creek and the surrounding areas in a tidal wave of snow and ice not experienced in a decade.

Yeah, right.

Knitting needles jabbed through my skull behind my eyes, scraping sparks from the bone. My face screwed up, battling the lancing pain as I stumbled from the elevator, dragged by Maggie, as she towed me down the short hallway toward her breakfast adventure feast.

Great. Another skull-splitting migraine. A screaming fun park roller coaster I hadn't ridden since fleeing from Ruby Creek.

I stammered to an uncertain stop at the border where carpet met tile. Lightning flashed behind my eyes, blinding me for an instant. I lost my balance, tumbled against a wall, thankful for its solidity as I pinched the bridge of my nose and tossed whispered curses.

Maggie yanked my hand with growing impatience, her bubbling exuberance degenerating into the six-year-old version of mob mentality.

"Hurry up, Mommy," she said. "Before they're all gone."

Her whiny tone grated against my nerves, kindling flames that threatened a firestorm. I jerked my hand from hers, clutched my head, wishing the throbbing agony would die or at least dwindle to a class five hurricane.

Maggie continued to jerk the hem of my baggy flannel shirt.

"Give Mommy a moment, baby. Please," I said through gritted teeth.

The jerking continued, more subdued, but insistent.

"Hurry, Mommy, hurry," she said. "They're going to run out and you promised that I could have one."

I looked down at her, my brow furrowed between the unrelenting sledgehammer pounding my skull and Maggie's insistence.

"What are they going to run out of?" I asked as she pried me from the wall and marched me through a maze of milling bodies and over-crowded tables into the breakfast buffet area.

"You promised I could have a belching waffle this morning. With whipped cream and strawberries, and lots and lots of syrup. Is it round? It has to be round. Belching waffles aren't allowed to be square. I won't like it if it's square. And it has to have all of those little square thingies inside it. If it doesn't have them, it's a pancake. And you know I don't like pancakes."

"But you love pancakes," I said, trying to ignore the iron spikes pounding into my brain.

Maggie growled, scrunched her face into a scowl, and crossed her arms. "You promised I could have a belching waffle, Mommy. You promised."

I looked down at her, my head throbbing, brain whipped into an oozing mush. Was this what it was like to be a normal six-year-old girl, whose immediate life crisis was triggered by Belgian waffles with whipped cream, strawberries, and too much fake maple syrup? My irritation melted, the searing agony beating the back of my skull slowing to a low simmer.

I nodded, afraid of the building tears that would spill over the top of the dam if I said the words.

Giving me a dubious stare, she grabbed my hand, dragged me toward the waffle maker hunkering against the back wall, sandwiched between untidy lines of whipped cream cans and plastic crates of mushy strawberries, gooey blueberries, and slivered almonds.

My stomach heaved.

My mind twisted, tossing a bleeding memory onto the dinner table. Pancakes for dinner. Dad working in his office. Again. Mom's burgeoning irritation and anxiety. The constant ringing of her phone. Her refusal to answer it. The silent, whispered words urging me from the table, propelling me to her secret place where she'd hidden the pictures taken of her with her special friend. The voices, insistent and eager, as I gave the envelope to my dad.

I bit the inside of my cheek.

"Mommy?"

"Since when don't you like pancakes?"

The worry creasing her brow smoothed away. "Don't be silly, Mommy," she said. "You're the one that doesn't like pancakes."

"But—" Confusion ricocheted through my brain.

The discordant buzz of jumbled conversation cavorted with the dull scrape of cheap plastic flatware against cheap paper plates. I stood in front of the waffle maker, snorting the sweet stench of cheap waffle mix and fake maple syrup. Half-baked batter clung to the rounded iron edges, oozed down the sides, forming cream-colored pustules on the stained white counter linoleum.

"Are you sure about this?"

She stood beside me, shifting from foot to foot, her growing impatience propelling me into making a round belching waffle that I didn't remember promising she could have.

Chair legs scuffed and scratched at the dining area floor, digging trenches through my sluggish thoughts, twin siblings to the blood-soaked memories from the cemetery yesterday.

Maggie reached for the waffle maker.

I slapped her hand away. "Don't do that! You could burn yourself."

Maggie drew back.

Sudden shame drowned my rage.

I scooped her into my arms, hugged her, and buried my face into the nape of her neck. "I'm sorry, baby. I didn't mean to snap. It's...this place."

"The hotel?"

"No, baby," I said. "Not the hotel."

She hugged my neck, squeezing hard enough to pull a grimace out of me.

I kissed her cheek and set her down. "Do you forgive me?"

"Of course I forgive you," she said. "As long as I get my belching waffle. And don't forget, it has to be round." She stood on her toes, leaned toward the waffle maker. "Do they come with the tiny squares inside?" she asked. "You know I like those. They hold my syrup."

I chuckled, ruffled her uncombed, night-tangled hair.

The waffle maker beeped.

I pried Maggie's waffle from its mold, tried not to mangle it too much as I dumped it onto her plate, buried it in the weeping and mushy strawberries, drowned it in a lake of sugary brown goo, making sure I filled every crevice before slathering it in an ocean of whipped cream.

We wound our way through the last of the breakfast chaos. I dumped Maggie into an empty, sort of clean booth near the back of the dining area, set the disheveled waffle mess in front of her, and fell into the seat beside her, wondering if she'd allow me to grab a cup of crappy hotel coffee.

She glared at the round, pock-marked monstrosity and picked at the bedraggled edges with her fork.

"What?" I asked her, stabbing my fork into the edge, tearing a piece free and shoving it into my mouth. "It's full of sugary and whipped creamy goodness. What's not to like?"

She made a face, impaled the waffle through its heart. "It's gross," she said as she shoved the plate away. "I don't want it."

I sighed, pulled the plate back, forced another bite into my mouth. "C'mon, sweety. You need to eat something. We're going to be gone for a long time. It's delicious. See?" I opened my mouth to display the mostly eaten waffle mess stuffed inside.

She pouted, arms crossed, and leaned back in the seat. "It's gross," she said. "You're gross. I don't like gross. I can't eat gross."

My temper rose, a ratty image of my mom peeking through the fog, rage corkscrewing across her blood-spattered face as she touched the revolver to the side of her head. I stomped it down, slammed the door closed before it could slither back out from the dark.

"C'mon," I said. "Take three big bites. I'll let you go swimming again if you do."

She smacked me with a sideways look, calculated distrust behind her eyes. "You promise?"

"Pinky swear."

"Emmie Daugherty?"

The one Ruby Creek voice besides Daisy Pellerman's I had hoped to never hear again punched through the jumble of bad high school memories I kept hidden in the pockets of regret and remorse.

I looked up, pulled my mouth into a tremulous smile, doing a piss-poor job of masking my sudden, mixed emotions.

Danni McMillan, my high school junior on-and-off again lust crush, stood beside our table, towering over us, his slim, clean-limbed shadow gliding over the waffle.

Damn, he looked good. Embraced seductively in a tailored dark gray pinstripe suit, white shirt, and matching tie, his boyish grin and sun-bright, acid-washed blue-jean eyes pulling me back to my junior year and the crap we did under the football field bleachers. Before my fractured and defiant world went to hell.

He'd been my first. My best, until time and mileage driven by guilt and regret rewrote that history. Happy times.

I hadn't been his first. Or his last. Although I'd hoped I'd been his best. Bursting bubbles soaked my memories as I stared up into his eyes.

I cleared my throat and pursed my lips, unable to stomp down the sudden yearning crawling from my eyes.

How long had it been?

Nine damned years.

You'd think a messed-up girl with paralyzing childhood trauma issues would get over a guy skank like Danni McMillan after nine years. Especially after getting knocked up by the wolf of her dreams after escaping Ruby Creek.

Guess not.

A sour taste splashed across the back of my throat, poisoned the undecided smile slitting my mouth. The high school girl yearning that leaped from my eyes jumped to its death.

"Shit, it is you, isn't it?"

I smacked him with a scornful glare.

His gaze flicked to Maggie. He cleared his throat. "Sorry." He slid into the bench seat across from us, pulled the front of his suit jacket across his chest, but not before I noticed the holster strapped beneath his left shoulder and the butt of the pistol peeking out from it. He placed his hands on the table.

No ring. And no tan line on that finger. Not that either meant much. Not after my adventures in Denver.

"Join us, why don't you."

His smile faltered, found its footing before my next quivering heartbeat.

"Danni McMillan," I said, my voice even and a little icy.

"How long has it—"

"Nine years," I said.

He slid an anxious gaze toward Maggie.

"Hey there," he said, looking at me. "Who's this?"

"She's not yours."

He blew out a slow, small breath. Relief followed. Of course.

"She's six," I said. "It's been nine years since I left Ruby Creek." I leaned forward, hands clasped on the tabletop. "You can do math, can't you?"

His face burned red. "Yeah, sorry...I didn't mean—"

Of course you did.

"It's all good," I said, waving away his listless apology. "You never were the sharpest tool in the shed. But that's not why I liked you."

Another flashing blush.

This was new. The Danni McMillan I remembered would never have embarrassed so easily. Especially around me or any of the other five or six girls in his stable during our semester together. Before I fled the cloying suffocation of Ruby Creek and the almost twelve years of judgmental stares and gossip.

"What's your name?" he asked Maggie.

She frowned at him, jaw masticating a bite of syrup-soggy waffle. "I'm not allowed to talk to strangers," she said, tearing off another piece of waffle and shoveling it into her mouth.

I smiled, pride puffing my chest. That's my baby.

"Danni, this is my daughter, Maggie. Maggie, this is Danni. He's...an old friend from when Mommy lived here."

Danni nodded, tried his best disarming smile, reached across the table to shake her hand.

Maggie stared back, chewing, unimpressed, eyes judging.

He reclaimed his hand.

"Do you like round belching waffles?" Maggie asked, opening her mouth wide to display the gooey mound of ABC waffle stuffed inside.

I laughed. Would have spewed milk from my nose if I'd been drinking any.

Danni did his best deadpan, snorted a chuckle, and snagging my fork, crammed an elephantine piece of the sodden waffle mess into his mouth, gaped it open long enough to make sure Maggie saw the mishmash inside.

Maggie giggled, shoved in another bite. "I like him. He's funny."

"How the hell have you been?" he asked, glanced at Maggie, remembering to look chagrined for an instant before claiming another gigantic bite off Maggie's plate.

I hesitated, uncertain how to respond, not knowing if I wanted to answer. Instead, I stabbed my gaze at the telltale bulge under his left arm. "Join the cowboy mafia, did we?"

"What?"

"You're packing."

"How'd—"

"You forget who raised me?"

"No...I—" He shook his head. "I'm...interim chief. Just promoted. Until—" He hesitated, uncertainty glinting from his eyes.

I expected Sam to take some time off to bury Daisy and to mourn. But this? Didn't sit right somehow. The Danni McMillan I'd known ran in the opposite direction of responsibility. What had changed? I studied him, tried to decipher the conflicting emotions sprawling across his face.

I sipped my water. "A little young, aren't we? Are you even potty trained yet?"

He pinched his lips, refusing to meet my probing gaze. He toyed with his fork, looping whip-creamed syrup through the tines. "It's been hard on him," he said. "Losing Daisy like that." The words tumbled out, splattered themselves over the table. He looked at me, leery, as if I might try to stab him with Maggie's fork. "I'm the only full-time staff...you know, paid by the city. Everyone else—" His face reddened. "The mayor...she thought—"

"Hey, no need to explain anything to me. I don't live here anymore. Congrats."

Unsettled silence. "Thanks."

"What about you?" he said. "Doing anything exciting to put food on the table for you and the little miss?"

Lies paraded through my thoughts. He studied me, the same look he'd used when we were hot and horny teens under the bleachers. We'd been terrible liars to each other, always knowing the truth from fiction when it spilled out. Watching him, I realized I wouldn't be able to lie to him now. I fished a business card from my shirt pocket, slid it across the table.

He arched a brow as he picked it up. "A bounty hunter?"

"I prefer independent fugitive recovery agent," I said.

"Are you any good?"

My turn to arch a brow. "Do we look like we live in my car?"

"Touché." He slid the card back.

"Keep it," I said. "You never know when you might need the services of a damn good independent fugitive recovery agent."

"In Ruby Creek?"

I shrugged.

"Done!"

I looked at Maggie. She beamed at me, syrup clinging to her hand as it dripped down off her fork, maple-stained whipped cream smeared across her mouth.

"Can we go swimming now?"

I dabbed the edge of a paper napkin into my water glass, used it to peel the top layer of syrupy goo from her hand and mouth. "Tonight, baby. After we're done saying goodbye to—" I slid a look toward Danni. "Gramma Daisy."

She frowned. "Okay. Can we invite Grampa Sam to swim with us tonight?"

A sudden chill dragged clawed fingers down my back. I glanced at Danni. Nothing. Just a wilted sadness dripping from his gaze.

"Thought that's what might have brought you back. Didn't think it had anything to do with me, or..." He tapped my card. "The independent fugitive recovery business."

He at least had the decency to flash a lopsided smile at his poor joke. The well-aimed jab pricked my heart.

"We've gotta go," I said as I slid from the booth, dragging Maggie out by her sticky hand.

Danni reached over, touched my arm. "Can we talk?" he asked. "Later. Maybe after?"

I hesitated, thought I might try the lie this time. "We're leaving as soon as it's done," I said. "No real reason to linger."

His eyes narrowed, and I knew he knew.

But instead of the probing questions, he said, "Sure," slid from the booth and buttoned his jacket. "No worries. Maybe in another nine years." He paused. "Or when Maggie graduates college." He winked at Maggie. "Nice to meet you, little miss."

She smiled back, hid behind me, her tiny fists tangled in the hem of my drooping flannel.

I reached out, but he had already turned and was striding away, waving good morning to the desk staff. He didn't turn back before he vanished through the sliding glass doors, leaving me with nothing except for the vague, wafting scent of Brut Fabergé, the same fragrance I remembered from high school.

Sam Pellerman

Sam sat in his police SUV, the heater spitting hot air from the dashboard vents. The wipers clacked a precise tempo against the windshield, the rhythmic thumping soothing the storm brewing behind his eyes. He sipped bourbon from his thermos, an anniversary gift from Daisy when he'd been promoted to chief twenty-five years ago.

He spied the telltale outline of a canary yellow backhoe, the fouled claw resting beside an open grave.

Daisy's grave.

Her glossy platinum and silver-plated bronze casket waited in the funeral home basement, sterile light reflecting off the burnished metal surface. Ready to be dropped into the hole later this afternoon, the gaping void filled with frozen, ice-grimed dirt. The headstone would have to wait for spring. Backhoes were great for digging graves in arctic-hard ground. Not so much for setting a granite headstone.

He snorted, sipped his bourbon, wondered again what the hell he was doing here. To draw out the Quixote and end this nightmare. Why else, you moron?

He fingered the detonator nestled in the pit of his coat pocket, wondered again if he'd wired enough explosives to the undercarriage of his SUV to blow the Quixote to hell. For good.

Daisy intruded on his morose thoughts.

God, he had loved that woman hard, even after she torched every-thing he'd believed in and wanted, driving Emmie from their lives before she'd had the chance to grow into a proper woman. Too young when she left. Too angry. Too hard and closed off from everyone, except Daniel McMillan. Another nail in that coffin.

He slurped more bourbon, wiped sweaty frost from his window. Damned defrost was sleeping on the job again. Or maybe he'd just become a heavy breather.

Forgiveness for Daisy's unsympathetic treatment of Emmie came hard. Day by day. Hour by hour. Sometimes, not at all. Hell, he didn't know. But something changed between them when he brought Emmie into their lives; a wall was built, brick by brick, between them and their relationship that neither of them could completely breach. Not that Daisy seemed to want to tear those bricks down.

Through the years, he'd hoped that Daisy would accept Emmie. She never did. Daniel McMillan became the proverbial straw that broke that camel's back.

"Make a choice," Emmie demanded the night before she left. "You can't have it both ways. Not anymore. Not after this."

Guess he'd made his choice.

And Emmie had gone, everything she owned stuffed into the back of her GMC Terrain, including, unknown to her, the cornerstone of her blood-strewn foundation. He'd watched her drive away, not even a wave goodbye. From either of them.

Seventeen damned years old, going on thirty-five. But still so damned young.

And that was that.

Only that wasn't that.

Forgive and forget. Daisy did neither.

Blame came easily enough. A little girl, the spitting image of the woman who murdered Daisy's twin brother. Too many reminders. Too much remembrance. An innocent six-year-old girl caught in the crossfire of that nightmare. Daisy did the only thing she knew how to do. She pushed the chick from the nest.

Fly or die.

Emmie had flown, despite her broken wings.

Before he could figure out how to make it right, Alzheimer's blasted into their lives. Quick and insidious, it chewed Daisy away bite by grizzly bite until nothing remained. No compassion. No grace. No respite. He took a breath, and she was gone. Her mind was cold and dead, waiting for him to cut the cord and let her go.

Damned hardest decision he'd ever made. But he'd done the right thing. He knew that. Still, the guilt nibbled at his soul, peeling off scraps and splinters. His nightmares crammed to bursting with visions of her accusing gaze punching holes through his heart as her body gasped its final breaths.

He'd had nine years to figure out how to keep Emmie away forever.

And then Daisy died. Deep in his heart, he'd known Emmie would come back. Not for Daisy, but for him. And the Quixote and his Sancho made sure of it.

He emptied the thermos, belched, and winced, expecting Daisy to scold him for his lack of manners. The quiet hum of the heater answered him, but didn't scold. Guess it was too strung out to care, either.

He clicked on the radio. A Marvin Gaye song he didn't recognize. He had no use for ol' Marvin, but Daisy loved the guy, made her weak between her knees every time. Turned out to be a blessing for him. Not so much for Deacon Barrett.

A feather of stuffy, sulfur-hot air tickled the back of Sam's neck.

About damned time.

The passenger door opened. A tall, gaunt figure bundled in a coal-black leather duster and soot dusty fedora slid into the seat beside him. The Quixote flashed a cheshire cat grin and tipped the brim of his hat as he closed the door, fiery red eyes pulsating. "Samuel."

Sam reached for his service weapon.

A pallid, emaciated hand gripped his wrist, talon-like fingers grinding bone.

Sam grunted, leaned over, his hand spasming open. The pistol clattered to the floor.

"You do me an injustice, Samuel, believing that you could deny me the justice owed by the families that stole my life and my future."

Sam massaged his wrist, glanced down at the pistol where it lay impotent on the floor between them. "You're the Quixote. And you're here to kill me."

The flicker of a knowing smile. "True enough. But I believe a more civilized conversation is in order before we resort to violence. Would you not agree?"

"No."

An amused snort. "A pity, to be sure. And a regret that we have not yet managed to evolve past our baser instincts for destruction and savagery."

"What the hell do you want?"

A lamented sigh. "To speak to you of your dear and departed wife, Daisy."

Sam tensed, the anguish strangling his heart, twisting the knots tighter. He gripped the steering wheel, shook his head. "No," he said. "You don't get to talk about her."

A lifted brow stretched desiccated flesh above a glowing eye. "But I am the reason your beloved currently languishes in hell." He peered at Sam with feigned concern. "Do you not wish to know the agonies her soul suffers because of her uncharitable attitude toward Emerson, the future love of my life?" He chuckled. "Who I must thank you for bringing back to me, despite her soiled nature. Her dear, dear daughter, Maggie, however—"

"I found Tristan Daugherty's journal."

A pause. "Did you, now? How delightful." He winked. "It is quite an exciting read, if you ask me. A real page-turner, I believe, is the term." A quiet laugh, the rueful shake of the skeletal head. "Master Daugherty had quite the flair for the dramatic. And I should know."

A hand reached in, yanked the breath from Sam's chest. He gasped, blinked tears from his eyes.

"A reminder that you do not know half as much as you think you do, and far less than you should."

Cold air washed over him, froze his breath as he exhaled. He shivered, clenched the steering wheel, his knuckles showing white.

Sam felt the weight of an arm draped across his shoulder.

"Now, where were we? Ah yes, Daisy's current torturous predicament."

"I know how to destroy you," Sam said.

"And you believe this knowledge will save you and the others?" An amused twinkle that glimmered in the burning eyes. A smirk lifting the corner of his mouth. "An amusing thought." He leaned over, his febrile breath sweeping over Sam's face. "Your ancestor tried once to destroy me. He and his dear lady love burned in their home instead, standing amidst the flames watching, while I took their daughter's soul." He leaned back, reached into his duster, set the book on Sam's lap. "Perform what mischief you may," he said.

Sam pulled the detonator from his coat pocket, pressed the button. A red light blinked. "Dead man's switch," he said.

Scorn rolled across the Quixote's face. He shook his head, expression dripping with sorrow as he clicked his teeth. "Samuel," he said, "how disappointing. I expected more from you. I do, however, believe that a dead man's switch is appropriate in the moment."

The weight across his shoulders vanished.

Sam's throat constricted. He gasped. Amusement passed over the Quixote's face as he crushed Sam's trembling hand and the detonator.

Throbbing pain erupted in his chest, hounded by a building pressure pushing against his ribs. Agony slid a white-hot knife blade into his shoulder, through his neck and jaw, rattling his teeth before slicing down his arm.

He lurched forward, slapped a fist into the steering wheel, eyes bulging, retched a breath before sagging sideways against his window, eyelids fluttering.

The Quixote tipped the brim of his fedora. "Good morrow, Samuel," he said. "I do hope you encounter your beloved Daisy within the depths of whatever hell you shall inhabit. It has been a pleasure."

The Quixote

I GRAZED THE BACKS of my fingers down the side of Linda Griffith's face, toyed for a heartbeat with matted and tangled corn-silk yellow hair at the cleft of her jaw. Not her natural color, but one that soothed her dilettante vanity.

A shame.

The silvering auburn-shaded hairs sprouting from her scalp more suited her demeanor and the illusory beauty she so desperately clung to. Her natural beauty would have continued to turn heads.

She shuddered at my touch, whimpers drooling from quivering lips. Blood dribbled from her nose, pooled at the top of her cupid's bow, ran down her face from gashes she'd dug into her flesh.

"Please," she whispered, voice quaking and thick with terror. She reached up, the nubs of her fingers clawing the air.

I stared down at her and the growing puddle between her splayed legs, tasted the reek of urine on the tip of my tongue. I squatted beside her, pressed a gentle kiss upon her cheek. "Do not worry," I said. "You shall have your peace. Soon."

Firelight cavorted with the dark, twisting and turning.

Another storm of whimpered cries. Hiccupped sobs jerking her body, the puppeteer flinging the marionette's limbs drunkenly through the shadows. She closed her eyes, her face screwed into a knot of dread.

I smoothed the clumps snarling her hair and stood, laid my hand on the top of her head, turned it toward the shivering body curled into itself against the opposite wall.

It rocked back and forth, knobby knees pressed into an emaciated chest, skinny arms snugged tightly around bony legs. Tormented whispers wept from chapped lips. Dingy light glinted from ferret-like, untinged eyes, hollowed and empty from a drugged stupor, sunken back into bruised, ghostly sockets.

"Your son," I said, voice razor-edged, "should not be this way, his soul rotted and stinking of death, his mind foul and fetid, thoughts twisted and obscene." I stroked her hair, curled my fist into the knotted strands, pulled her to her feet, her back scraping the wall. I stared into her eyes. Tears streamed from the corners, tumbled down her cheeks. Her mouth quivered, spewing spittle and bile.

I wiped the corners of her mouth with a ragged piece of linen, its white, luminescent shade smudged now blood red. "I take no pleasure in your torture, dear lady, but justice demands recompense, does it not?"

Guttural, mewling sounds oozed from her throat. She jerked a nod.

I snorted the reflection of a smile, shoved the besmirched rag into her hands, dropped her. She folded, coughing and sputtering, back pressed into the wall. The last few drops of my empathy evaporated.

I strode across the room, squatted beside Micah Griffith's body, the constable I had slain earlier. It leaned against the wall, tall, bullish frame slack, long, lanky legs extended, shriveled hands splayed negligently beside it, stiffened fingers curled and claw-like. A once vibrant face, bursting with a slow-burning rage, now grayish and tinged black, cheeks sunken and hollow, slack-mouthed, eyes clouded and empty.

"Your husband," I said. "Micah? We met earlier. When the day still breathed promise." My gaze wandered to the man huddled beside her.

The lover. The man to whom she had given herself when her marriage died. The same man responsible for the care and training of the mind and body of a ten-year-old girl who now awaited my rescue.

He bore no connection to my curse. And yet, justice demanded its recompense.

He met my glare, eyes knowing and accepting, expression grim, though tinged with fallen hope.

Four lives spoiled beyond redemption.

I allowed the woman to witness my sadness and disappointment, then reached into my coat pocket and dropped her husband's service pistol beside the boy.

"I am sorry. Truly." To the boy. "I grant you this opportunity to redeem your heart, soul, and mind in the sight of our almighty God."

I rose, strode from the room into a black, fathomless hall to the end, and a closed door. I grasped the door handle, shut my eyes.

Two gunshots echoed down the corridor, rattled the ceiling. A third followed. Silence, except for the faint whisper of my breath upon the door.

I pushed it open.

The young lady crowded into the far corner of the room, between a satin white, pine four-posted bed and teal-colored shuttered accordion closet doors. Tears streamed down her face, soaking the collar of her loose, gauzy blouse, knees drawn to her chest, spindly arms chained around shaking legs.

As I entered, she quieted, eyes growing round, lips quivering, the rest of her becoming rabbit still. *If I don't move, you can't see me.*

I sat upon the edge of the bed, opened my book, held it to her. She shrank back, eyes slick with tears. I offered the book again, hopeful.

"Do not fear," I said, my tone soothing and inviting. "This is for you. To keep you safe and unharmed. For us. Please."

She shook her head, cringed further back, the side of her face buried against the wall. She cried, her words chaotic and incoherent.

I continued to hold the book toward her, my hope waning, yet unwilling to die. She looked at me, and I viewed behind her eyes what had lain hidden before; the stain of sin tainting the edges of a soul beginning to molder and rot.

My hand jerked back, and I almost dropped the book. Now just my story, no longer ours. Tears welled, driven by anguish. Too late, I thought. Too late. Grief looped the hangman's noose about my victory.

I placed the book on the bed, knelt beside the girl, stroking her head with a gentle hand. I picked her up and laid her carefully on the bed. She shook, her limbs locked about her torso, cocooning her body. Continuing to stroke her hair, I uncoiled her limbs, one at a time, laying her flat against the quilted comforter draping the mattress. Comical images of a rabbit, skunk, and a foundling deer galloped across the embroidered white fabric, chased by fluttering bluebirds and butterflies.

Her chest heaved, her breath bursting from between her parted lips, sucked back into her quivering lungs, eyes round and black, the whites wiped away like chalk from a board.

She stared up at me, panic etched into the soft lines of her youthful face. "Don't hurt me."

I shuddered.

"I will not," I said. "Pain will no longer be your constant companion. That, I promise you." I tore her page from my book, its edges beginning to smolder and curl, set it at her shoulder, the shadowed outlines of an elvish face hovering on the brink of consciousness.

After sliding the fluffed feather pillow from under her head, I pressed it against her face.

Emerson Daugherty

I PARKED IN FRONT of the house I grew up in, a house I thought I would never see again. The dingy white bi-level squatted near the back of a half-acre lot, grass lawn, cracked concrete driveway, bordered by red brick pavers that wound their way to the steps of a poured concrete front porch. Uncurtained dual-paned windows overlooked the cul-de-sac that curved in a half-moon circle, a safe place for a child to play.

A light, powdery snow wafted through the afternoon air. The cloud-crowded sky hovered low to the ground, deciding how much more snow to dump as it pulled shadows across the ground like saltwater taffy.

A jumble of tire tracks plowed through the snow carpeting the drive, vanishing behind the closed garage door.

Coming or going? I wasn't sure which I preferred.

I sat, staring, hands clutching the GMC's wheel, trepidation twisting my stomach and jumbling my thoughts. It had been nine years since I fled Daisy Pellerman and Ruby Creek. I didn't get far, spent most of my time lurking around Denver and Colorado Springs. I met a man I thought would heal my bleeding wounds, salve my scars.

Instead, he bled me more, carved more scars across my heart and soul. One good thing came out of that relationship, though. I looked in the rear-view mirror, smiled at Maggie as she stared out her window from her car seat.

"Is that Grampa Sam's house?" she asked.

"It is," I said. "It's the house I grew up in."

"It looks kind of scary."

An unnatural gloom peered from the windows of the house, saturating the drifting snow with a spreading murkiness. I shivered, goose pimples snaking down my spine and shoulders. I dragged Tristan Daugherty's journal from the passenger seat, clutched it in my lap.

"I don't think I want to go in there," Maggie said, her voice quivering. "I don't think grampa Sam is home." She sat up in her car seat, eyes bright with sudden mischief. "We should go back to the hotel and go swimming. Maybe he'll be home tomorrow."

I smiled, veiled by the misgivings that picked at my resolve. We were uninvited. Sam didn't know I'd come back. Not yet. Hadn't tried to find me, to tell me about Daisy's death. Not that I was eager to pay my last respects. Despite the circumstances of my coming to live with Sam and Daisy Pellerman, she had made my life a living hell until driving me from their home and Ruby Creek the week after I turned seventeen.

She'd called it shoving the chick from the nest. Fly or die. The law of the wild. I'd called it bitterness and revenge for something I hadn't done and had no control over. I had known little about my dad's murder or my mom's suicide, and I'd preferred to leave as much of my ignorance intact as I could.

The constant nightmares that had plagued me were bad enough. Living under the ire of a woman I wanted to like, and whom I wanted to love me, became too much to bear.

Sam had other plans.

Not that I'd cooperated with those plans, not while I was growing up under his roof. Somehow, he'd known the truth. About every damned thing. He'd tried to tell me. Tried to warn me, to prepare me. Exhausted by my recalcitrance, he tried to protect me.

And he never gave up.

I had discovered the Daugherty journal stuffed into the bottom of a box of wadded-up clothes a week after I found a dump with a ratty bed and running water to call home. It sat in the bottom of that box for another week while I argued with myself about what I was going to do with it. I lost the argument.

Trepidation pumped my heart the first time I touched the aged and cracked leather binding, raking my fingertips over the brittle paper as I turned the pages, the once bright parchment dull and yellowed, the ink flat and lusterless.

Night terrors crouched on my shoulders for a week after that. I woke, screaming, sweat drenching my hair, plastering my night shirt to my body. My neighbors groused and griped, harassed me in the halls, left me thoughtless gifts at my door. A group threatened to have me evicted. But I had paid, in cash and in advance, and had included a generous bonus for a no-questions-asked long-term arrangement. A silent gift from Sam. He'd also gifted me another, smaller provision for those uncommon and awkward moments when words failed, and you couldn't run away. A gun.

My neighbors left me in grudging peace after they discovered I was packing and knew how to use my little friend.

Another month slid down the toilet before I unearthed my page hidden in the back of the journal, jammed between Sam's scrawled notes.

I checked my watch, looked at the foreboding lightless windows of my childhood home. Maybe the Ruby Creek gossip telegraph had been quicker than I expected. Maybe Sam knew I'd come back. Maybe he'd decided he didn't want to see me. Or couldn't see me. Maybe what I needed was to take Maggie back to the hotel so she could swim and just screw the whole funeral and death thing, get the hell out of Ruby Creek tomorrow morning, and back to Denver, and our lives.

But Daisy's funeral was an excuse, not the reason I had come back to Ruby Creek. I had unfinished business with a one-hundred-thirty-year-old revenant that had stolen my family and my life, if not my soul. And I needed Sam Pellerman to help me close the cover on that book. I needed him to keep my Maggie safe while I tore the heart from our curse and burned it to ash.

A fractured memory tugged at my thoughts, whispered, "Come inside. We've been expecting you."

I blinked, my mouth gone dry. The dark and empty windows continued to leer. Snow fell in rainy sheets, white pebbles bouncing off asphalt and concrete.

Maggie was right. The house did look scary.

"Hey, baby girl," I said, looking into the rear-view mirror at an empty car seat and an open door.

Snow swirled in through the opening, dusting the floor and seat with a grungy white powder. A stilted wind tapped the door, creaking the hinges and swaying the car as if rocking an infant to sleep.

Panic stabbed me, twisting the knife blade until I couldn't breathe.

A hushed, noxious chuckle rattled through my brain, snapping at the heels of my thoughts, urging them into a frenzied dance, spinning, and spinning, and spinning, and spinning.

My breath frosted the windshield.

How long had I been zoned out?

How the hell had Maggie—?

The GMC sputtered and died.

"Maggie!" I spilled out of the car, knees and hands ramming into ice-slimed concrete, the jarring impact popping my right shoulder and crunching my right knee. My right arm and leg collapsed, and I dove face-first into the snow and ice. I inch-wormed my way forward, left hand scrabbling at ice-brittle grass, left foot shoving against dirt-riddled snowpack, dragging the right side of my body behind.

Dead weight.

"Maggie!" The wind snatched my cry. Ice water soaked my gossamer blouse and trendy black, silky slacks, welding them to my frigid body, too numbed to even shiver.

Antarctic wet T-shirt contest, anyone?

I mopped the snow from my eyes, stared across the frozen landscape, snaking toward the front of the house. A trail of wandering child-sized footprints zigzagged through the powdery carpet, vanished at the porch steps. The front door gaped open, swinging on groaning hinges, knocking against the frame in a fitful beat.

"Mommy?"

Maggie's quiet voice crooked a finger at me from inside the house, inviting and tranquil, but quivering with a delighted, psychotic anticipation.

"Maggie," I bawled, left arm reaching out, hand stretching, fingers grasping. "Mommy is coming, baby girl." My arm gave out, slapped into the snow. My head followed, numbing cold enveloping my face. Tears froze to my skin, stung the nerves, lighting them with fire.

"Well, now, isn't this just the cat's meow?"

Crunching snow and ice pelted me.

The abrupt taste of shivering air against the side of my head from a kneeling body. I lifted my face from its freezing husk, blinked water from my eyes.

An age-whittled face, puffy with grief, ogled me.

"Sam—?"

He snickered and winked. "Not...quite. But this isn't about me now, is it?" The face rose, milky eyes scanning the swirling shroud. "The witch is waiting for you inside. She's not really happy that you're here." The vacant eyes swiveled down. "Truth be told, Daisy's been quite the curmudgeon since she kicked the bucket, carping and screaming from dusk till dawn. Won't give me a decent night's sleep." An awkward pause. "Her behavior's been a little embarrassing, if you ask me."

"Who—?"

Cold, stinging breath patting my cheek. Transparent, dead eyes looking into mine. The hint of a demented smile.

"C'mon, Emmie, is that all you've got? After the pig's breakfast you've endured these past twenty years? I'll admit, I'm just a tad disappointed that my play-act daughter grew up to be a wimp and not the stalwart young woman I meant her to be. My fault, I guess. Can't trust anyone to raise your kids these days, can you?"

Shifting snow, scratching the side of my face. My head dropped back into its reverse snow cone.

"So that's it, is it? No fighting to the bitter end? No staring death in the face and telling it to go to hell?"

I moaned.

"Fine, I'll be the dad...for once. But don't get used to it."

Raw, numbing hands grasped my right wrist and yanked.

I howled, torment slicing through my shoulder as I was dragged through the snow and dumped at the base of the porch steps.

Footsteps strutted up the icy concrete.

"You're on your own for the rest of the journey, princess. Don't dillydally. Everyone's waiting for your grand entrance, especially that super cute little bundle of joy you popped out six years ago."

A rasping chuckle grated my nerves, scraping the ends raw.

Another moan. I lifted my head, focused bleary eyes on the concrete peak at the top of the steps. A wavering haze shrouded the gaping maw, sucking light and matter into the void. My breath shuddered, my dislocated shoulder throbbing. Ragged lightning bolts slashed across my vision.

I reached up with my left hand, grabbed the iron railing, levered my left leg beneath me, dumped my butt on the first step.

"Mommy?"

Maggie's eager, enthusiastic voice propelled me upward. My left foot found the concrete, my left arm vise-gripped the porch railing. Pull. Hop. Grit teeth. Don't pass out. Wash. Rinse. Repeat.

I leaned against the railing on the porch, heaving air, supporting my dead weight on my left foot, peered into inky nonexistence. "Maggie?"

Haunting silence.

I shoved off the rail, hopped through the doorway...into hell.

Daisy slouched in a hackberry dining room table chair, head lolling, eyelids pinned to her brows, barren sockets glowering, stockinged legs splayed apart, swollen feet popping the seams on her dull, black leather heels.

Sam knelt beside the chair, a blue-veined hand squeezing Daisy's. A leprous, creamy liquid leaked from her distended and bloated fingertips.

Behind her stood the hackberry dining room table that had ruled the chairs, leaning cockeyed against the shattered liquor cabinet, ragged splinters torn from the edges, and tossed about the room.

The cabinet doors sat near the alcove, chiseled glass plates shattered, sparkling grains strewn across the floor, twinkling in pools of spilled bourbon, scotch, and wine. Two more chairs, reduced to kindling, lay jumbled near a fractured table leg.

A shredded cardboard legal file box slumped against the table, torn manila folders, ransacked journals, and blood-soaked papers strewn across the floor, clawing their way back into the ruin of the crate.

My stomach heaved. My body buckled. Flashing spears shot through my eyes as my right knee struck the floor. I gasped and sputtered, spewing vomit over the tiles.

"Emerson."

I jerked my head up. My vision swam, and Daisy's pasty face danced a jigsaw puzzle jig, pieces rearranging to form a new picture.

She glowered at me from the chair, disapproval plastered to her pallid face, her cheeks hollow, skin sallow, eye sockets dribbling slimy goo. She frowned, bloodless lips sagging downward to touch her chin.

"Maggie?" I croaked. "Where's my daughter?"

"You don't deserve to be a mother."

The coarse, sandpaper voice backhanded me. I sagged to the floor, panting.

"You're a common whore, spreading your legs for anything lewd enough to leer at you. The feral spawn of an adulteress, murderer, and suicide. You're not fit to breathe the same air as the precious, innocent soul you thrust into the world."

"Stop," I said, my voice quivering. "Please, stop."

A wicked cackle rattled my bones. "Stop? Why? Have I offended your self-righteous sensibilities? Thrown your virtue into the offal and stomped it into a wriggling mass of crap?"

A lull. The air coiling slimy tentacles around me, constricting, crushing my chest.

"I think not. Virtue is not a characteristic of your foul nature."

"Mommy?"

"Maggie! Baby! Mommy's here. Where are you?"

Dull, scraping laughter.

The scratching slide of a heavy object over the floor. It spun through the sea of vomit, spitting puke into my face. A semi-automatic pistol. Police-issued. Sam's service weapon.

I raised my head.

Pitch-black cavities stared back, trickling malice. "Whore. Tart. Prostitute. Hooker. Floozy. Jezebel. Trollop. Tramp." The nod of a wilting chin. "Pick it up. Put that bullet in your brain. You know you want to. Been dreaming of it since your tramp mother killed my brother and offed herself. Go on, do it!"

I clenched my left fist. Drool drizzled from between my trembling lips. Rage seethed, wrung my gut, strangled my chest.

"Save your daughter from the hell of your own pitiful existence. Give her back the innocence you stole by continuing to breathe. Go on, blow your brains out. Save Maggie."

I picked the gun up in a shaking hand.

"Mommy?"

I screamed, raised the gun, fired three quick, successive rounds.

The body in the chair bucked, the head jerking. It slumped forward, rolled to the floor, flopped on its back, smoke tendrils corkscrewing into the air from the murky eye sockets. Sam stared, mouth gaping, scarlet blossoming across his chest from underneath his pressed, starch-white dress shirt. He toppled to the floor, lay beside Daisy's corpse.

I dropped the gun, shrieking, slimed myself across the floor, and wormed on top of Sam's body, buried my face into his bloody chest, and sobbed.

"Mommy, help me! Please!"

Daniel (Danni) McMillan

Danni McMillan stood in the hurricane's eye surrounding Sam Pellerman's dining room. Dark puddles of melted snow grimed the crimson-stained floor, marking a gruesome battlefield of deformed and grotesque footprints scattered across the wooden planks. The moldering stench of eviscerated flesh hung heavy and silent, its weight an invisible presence ogling the wreckage strewn through the room.

Quiet, hesitant voices shimmied in uneasy circles around him, reaching out to touch, cringing back, burned by the scorching heat of his turmoil. Eyes watched, slinked away at his scathing glances.

Brilliant, colorless light blazed from floodlights circling the periphery of the dining room. Electronic flashes blinked through the blazing light, unmasking the gloom clinging to the room's corners.

Danni chewed his lower lip, thoughts roiling, hands hanging at his sides, clenching his notebook and pen, sweat sucking the inside of his black nitrile gloves to his skin. He stared at the mangled hackberry dining room table leaning against the shattered liquor cabinet.

Two chairs, reduced to kindling, lay jumbled near a fractured table leg, waiting only for a lit match to set the scene ablaze. Shards of glass glittered in the blinding light, reflecting a lurid rainbow onto the dusky walls. A shredded cardboard legal file box slumped against the table, torn manila folders, ripped journals, and blood-soaked papers strewn across the floor.

He looked at the two mangled bodies that lay side by side on the floor, heads hanging from twisted, shattered necks, faces pounded into tenderized meat, arms and legs yanked from their joints, arranged at impossible and unnatural angles.

One body wore a gore-spattered blue and violet patterned dress. The other, what might have been a black and gray pinstriped suit, white shirt, and matching tie.

What kind of rage did it take to desecrate human bodies like this? Trouble was, he knew. He'd seen that kind of rage before, nine years ago, pulsing through the nerves and blood of a girl he'd fallen for, despite his intention to just have some dangerous fun. You know? Walking a little too close to the edge for a little too long, without getting burned by the white-hot flame blazing in your face?

He'd known Emmie's history, the rumors that dogged her, the gossip and whispers that shadowed her every waking moment. The stares and glares from the other students, the callous pranks and jokes. Hell, who hadn't? The innocent Dulcinea that had survived the Quixote and his justice. If you believed in that kind of urban legend crap.

He hadn't. Still didn't.

His dad had warned him to stay away from that 'trouble.' He'd ignored him, leapt down the rabbit hole, believing himself immune to the bogeyman lurking at the bottom.

Instead, he'd become the moth that had flown too close to the firestorm and been burned to a cinder.

Still...

Danni drew in a long, shaking breath, belched bile into the back of his throat.

How the hell did you even sketch this scene?

A cleared throat beside him dragged his attention back to the macabre reality of the devastation gawking at him. Only, he wasn't laughing. And neither was anyone else.

Gale Henderson stood nearby, his aged and grizzled face invading Danni's personal space, dark eyes hooded in shadow, bulbous lips furled into a well-practiced grimace.

"I thought you retired," Danni said.

Henderson grunted. "I thought you were a wet-behind-the-ears high school dropout with delusions of grandeur."

"Graduated high school," Danni corrected.

Another grunt. "This unholy mess is a hell of a way to start a new tour."

Danni's gut twisted. He glanced at the carnage scattered around the liquor cabinet, pointed at the two bodies. "Tell me something about...them."

"They're dead."

Danni bit back a rending retort, pinched his brow with shaking fingers. "Then let's begin with the one in the dress."

Henderson paled. "Daisy's corpse, more than likely." He shuddered. "Called the mortuary. Someone broke in, took her body. Exact time of the...liberation is indeterminate."

Danni couldn't quell his shaking hand as he aimed his pen at the second body. "Is it him? Is it Sam?"

"I'm good. But no one is that good."

Danni blew out an agitated breath. "Cut the crap. Please." He looked at Henderson. "Is it Sam or not?"

Henderson shrugged. "Probably," he said. "Makes a nightmarish sort of sense. That kind of rage and resentment, building over a lifetime. It warps a person, especially someone who lived the kind of dysfunction that Emerson did." Another shrug. "Won't know for sure until the autopsy. But..." He held up a sealed plastic evidence bag. A gaudy gold ring glimmered from inside. "Forensics found this in a gooey pocket."

Danni peered at it, his gut kinking into another string of knots. Sam Pellerman's police chief's ring glowered back at him, the gold finish marred by crimson smears and bits of dull white flecks of bone.

"Shit."

"Yeah."

Despite the evidence sprayed across the scene and the fact that responding units discovered Emerson sprawled over what he presumed to be Sam's mutilated body, Danni couldn't believe that she had done this. Five-foot-four inches and a buck-forty-five, all lean muscle. She had the strength to drag Daisy Pellerman's corpse from the mortuary and drive it here, slop it into a chair...but then what? Had she already killed Sam? Or had she overpowered him and made him watch as she played out her psychotic episode of Family Feud?

None of it made any sense.

He sighed. "Any news on the Stanton Rest Stop deaths?"

Henderson shook his head, his expression somber, gray-whiskered, face pale. "Bobby Barrett and his wife, Becky, were found dead in the men's room. Bobby was beaten and stabbed multiple times. Becky slit her wrists with the box cutter we think she used to slice up Bobby. She did it right, bled out pretty fast." He pulled in a wobbly breath. "Then there's their little girl, Gracie. They found her sitting on a bench near a back corner. No visible signs of trauma, but—"

"What?"

Henderson sucked back a sob, wiped his nose with the back of his coat sleeve. He speared Danni with a terrified look. "Fifty damned years doing this… And only twice before…" His voice trailed off into an anxious silence.

Danni closed his eyes. Images of Bobby, Becky, and Gracie splattered across his thoughts.

Henderson stared, popping his jaw. "It's starting again, but way the hell worse this time."

"What's starting again?"

Tense silence.

Danni looked at him. "What's starting again?"

"The Quixote."

"Seriously?" Danni snapped his pen in two. Ink drooled onto his gloved fingers, stained the palm. He shoved the pieces into his trouser pocket, wiped his hand across his shirt, caught Henderson staring. "What?"

"Nothing."

"You don't actually believe in this urban family curse bull crap, do you?"

Henderson shrugged. "The rest stop victims were Barretts. Not a direct line. A one off. But they were Barretts."

Danni eyed him. "Starting a little early, isn't he? If the curse is real, wouldn't the Quixote have to wait until tomorrow to begin his rampage?"

"I don't make the rules."

"Unbelievable."

"You going to call the troopers?"

Danni laughed. "And tell them what? That the Quixote is back and on another generational slaughter?"

"It's in their files."

Danni huffed a breath. "Even if they stopped laughing long enough to send a unit, they can't get through. Both of the two lanes in and out of town are shut down because of the approaching storm. We're on our own." He glanced at Henderson. "I need that ID."

Henderson nodded. "We'll be transporting in a few. You'll know as soon as I know." He slapped Danni's shoulder. "Hell of a retirement party."

Danni watched Henderson shuffle out, shoulders slumped, the weight of his last case pressing him down. He turned back to the carnage, examined the mess, the papers and files littering the floor, mangled with blood and melted snow.

Robert Meadows, the current Ruby Creek high school chemistry and biology teacher and their forensics technician shambled by. Danni touched his shoulder. "You been through Emmie's GMC yet?"

Meadows shook his head. "No, not yet. Saving the ball-freezing fun for last."

"Mind if I take a look?"

"You're the boss."

Meadows set his forensics kit down, rummaged through the contents, began scattering colored plastic numbered tags through the slaughter surrounding the splintered dining room table.

Danni let himself out the front door.

Icy air assaulted him. He shuddered, hunched deeper into his parka. Occasional snowflakes wafted down from the gloomy sky, hovered before vanishing into the encroaching darkness. The stilted, unscented breeze ruffled his collar, toyed with his hair as he picked his way to the curb and Emmie's GMC.

The driver's side passenger door hung open, the backseat and child restraint chair strewn with a tattered blanket of glassy snow, the flakes glinting in the beam of his flashlight. The driver door leaned open as well, an impression of a fallen body plunged into the snow beside the curb.

Emerson or Daisy's corpse?

Careful not to disturb the impressions, wincing at the footprints he left behind, Danni skated around the car, tried the front and rear passenger doors. Both unlocked. He shined the beam of his flashlight through the front passenger window, the tip of the beam illuminating a leather-bound book on the floor beneath the front seat.

Frowning, he opened the door, scooted in, snagged the book from its half-assed hidey-hole, and opened the stiff and arthritic binding, cringing at the snap and crackle of the paper as he turned the pages.

He read a name, sucked in a quick, rasping breath, and closed the cover, his heart skipping behind his chest. What the—? He opened the volume again, lingered over the name scribbled across the first page, and the dates scratched into the parchment underneath. Leafing through the pages, he stopped to squint at the cramped writing crawling across the paper, the ink almost too washed out in places to decipher. He read the notes scratched into the margins, the hurried handwriting familiar, the ink darker and bold against the browning paper.

His radio crackled with static.

"Hey, McMillan, you online?" Walter Durham, the longest department veteran. Retired a couple of years ago. Now a volunteer.

Danni clicked the mike. "Yeah," he said. "Go ahead."

"You seen or heard from Micah?"

"No. Why?"

"No one has. Not since he rolled on a vagrant call at the elementary school this morning."

"Check with the Interlude?"

"Yeah. Nada."

"Call Sienna?"

"What do you think?"

Danni sighed. Sergeant Micah Griffith, his cousin, two or three times removed? A fifteen-year on-again-off-again veteran with Ruby Creek. An early rising star in the department. Until he wasn't. Now, a notorious drinker and womanizer known to vanish during his tour, usually for an extended liquid lunch at the Interlude, a 'gentleman's bar' at the edge of town, or to grab some rodeo time with his mistress, Sienna Ward. He always turned up, though, bedraggled and rumpled, but usually sober enough to finish his shift. He also always answered his radio, no matter his extracurricular activities.

Danni didn't need this. Not now. Not with this mess staring him down; Sam's corpse on its way to the morgue, Daisy's body on the gurney beside him. And Emerson Daugherty, the only person of interest, in the center of the storm.

"I'll check it out," he said. "Keep the boys focused. Let me know what they find."

"You think that thing was Sam?"

Chills frosted Danni's nerves. "I hope the hell not."

The Quixote

BLOOD SPLATTER PAINTED AN abstract crimson swath across the cream-colored dining room wall where I had nailed Paul Daugherty, a direct descendant of Tristan Daugherty, and a presumptive heir to the Daugherty empire. Delicate fingers of firelight danced across the sheen of blood. Tendrils of wood smoke wove gray white spiderwebs through the peaceful light and spread angelic wings above the twitching flames.

I sniffed the air, drew in the heady scents of cedar, mountain mahogany, and pinon pine, reveling in the hints of long-lost memories tickling the rent edges of driven purpose. I carried the remembrances as I would a babe in my arms, released them to join their fellows in the gathering dusk.

Lacey Daugherty, Paul Daugherty's wife, lay crumpled at my feet, the side of her head crushed in, clouded eyes staring blindly into the lengthening shadows. Accusation snarled through the space between us, worrying at my guilt and regret.

She was so like my blazing Nayara, swift to temper, the fierce lioness, yet harboring a tender and soothing soul. Riven too early from this world by the man sworn to cherish and protect her.

If I had arrived but a few moments earlier, before her husband had crushed her skull, she might yet still breathe, fire spitting fiercely from her chocolate brown eyes.

I knelt beside her, caressed the black hair, clotted and matted with blood, from her face. A scarlet sea soaked the ivory-white carpet beneath her smashed skull, the pile squishing under the fingers of my lambskin gloves; a gift from my blessed Nayara on the night our world ended.

A faint mewling came from my left

I licked the blood from my gloves, harpooned Paul Daugherty with a deadly stare, and grinned.

His eyes widened, threatened to roll back into his skull as he renewed his feeble attempts to escape his fate. He strained against the ten-penny nails spiking him to the wall, but collapsed after only a few measly seconds, his head lolling to kiss the top of his chest.

"Stay awake," I snapped.

His head jerked up, eyes fluttering open, gurgling a weak moan.

I retrieved a wooden baseball bat that lay beside Lacey Daugherty's mangled head, and stood, read the letters burned into the burnished maple: *Louisville Slugger*. I leered at the man nailed to the wall beside his own crimson-colored, abstract painting.

Louisville Slugger, indeed.

His eyes grew large as dinner plates as I approached, panicked grunts dribbling from his tongueless mouth. I set the bat down on the polished elm dining room table, its finish scraped and scratched raw by small, inquisitive hands. I stared at the scars, grief warring with admiration as I thought of my next Dulcinea, currently hiding inside the seat beneath the living room picture window.

I sighed, my wistful breath weighted with rage as I eyed Daugherty, marveling at the likeness to his original sire as I dragged the nail gun from the table.

Daugherty's struggles grew frenzied as I pressed the gun's muzzle against his chest over his heart. I stepped back.

He slumped against the nails pinning him to the wall, mewling cries scratching their way past his trembling lips. He craned his neck away, stared into the blankness of our tiny corner of the world.

"Look at me." I ground the tip of the nail gun into his chest, pressed gloved fingers into the wounds of a shattered shoulder.

His body contorted as he screamed.

"You, sir, are a cur. A coward. Undeserving of dignity or honor concerning the manner of your death."

He looked at me, the last embers of hope in his eyes burning to ash.

"I tell you true, sir, that I take no pleasure in what I must now do. But the soiled honor and dignity of your beloved Lacey demand the price I exact from you now." I put my lips to his ear and whispered. "Do you die with the honor you lacked in life?"

He soiled himself; the stink enveloping us.

I drew back, saddened by his cowardice.

And pulled the trigger. Once. Twice. Thrice.

I watched the light fade from his eyes.

Honor and love. Guilt and regret. All warred within me.

I dropped the nail gun at his feet, retrieved the bat from the table, knelt to press a last tender kiss upon Lacey Daugherty's parted lips.

A small noise from the living room snagged my attention.

I listened attentively, my rasping breath nearly silent in the still air. A faint scratching, clothing and hard-soled shoes dragged across roughened wood.

The child, Hollie. Hidden within the bowels of the window seat beneath the bay picture window in the living room.

"Dulcinea," I breathed.

I hitched the bat underneath my arm, strolled through the open doorway from the dining hall into the living room, whistling a dainty tune I had learned from Nayara while courting her.

The center of the scratched and scraped burnished oak floor lay hidden beneath a well-worn brown, tan, and pine-green fringed area rug littered with children's toys. The edges of the rug snuggled against the feet of a dark leather sofa, its arms caressing matching end tables.

Another whispered scrape, accompanied by a quiet and terrified gasp.

I paused, looked out the window at the falling snow. Twilight stretched through the wintry glass, spilled down from the window seat, clawed finger-like over the floorboards.

The scent of cinnamon and spice from a bowl of pot-potpourri invited me to relax, enjoy a cup of tea beside the fire as Nayara darned my socks and mended Dulcinea's Sunday dress. I closed my eyes, living once more in that world, content with my life, and eager to welcome our new child into the world.

An inferno erupted, trampling my peaceful remembrances beneath a stampede of thundering flames.

I swung the bat, striking a nearby lamp. Wood splintered. Glass shattered.

A shrill cry startled me into the present.

Chagrined by my folly, I propped the bat against the wall, sat carefully on the window seat beside its storage doors, and set the book in my lap. "Apologies, my little rose," I said. "I did not mean to frighten you beyond the terror you have already experienced."

A held breath greeted my statement.

I reached down, unlatched the door, and swung it open. Dread and its twin, Panic, slithered from the opening, tugging the strings binding them to the pocket-sized girl pressed against the back wall. Her trembling body vibrated against the elm paneling, ruffling the gauzy drapes drooping down the sides of the bay window.

"You may come out, little one," I said. "I will not harm you." I leaned over, stuffed my face into the opening, and grinned. "See, I am not half as horrifying as you may believe me to be."

She gulped and shrank back, her ice-blue eyes glinting in the half-light spilling through the doorway, lips quivering, auburn-streaked blonde hair disheveled, errant strands standing perpendicular.

I knelt on the floor, displayed my book to her, and reached in with a warmhearted hand. "I have a book with many exciting stories and adventures." I pushed it toward her. "I would very much like to read a few to you. Would you like that?"

She swallowed, her rabbit's gaze darting to the pages. A timid warmth spread through her eyes. She looked up, less distrustful, and nodded, her mouth puckered into a pout.

"Then I am afraid you must join me outside your elfin sanctuary, as I fear I am too bulky to fit inside with you." I made a half-hearted attempt to squeeze my considerable bulk through the narrow opening. I grunted and groaned, pretended to shoehorn myself into her crowded space. I gave up, sat back, and shrugged my shoulders.

"See?" I said. "I would need you to shrink me to your size before I could fit." I frowned. "Could you do that for me?"

She shook her head.

I sighed comically. "Then I see no other alternative." I brandished the book. "If you wish me to read you some stories from my book, you must join me outside your hole."

Hesitation, the last remnants of reticence and fear melting away. She unfurled her pint-sized body, crawled from her cave, the toes of her satin shoes scraping the wood.

I gathered her into my arms, sat her on my lap, and opened my book to an empty page.

"What do you see?" I asked.

A muted reply. "Nothing."

I raised my brows in shocked surprise, wiggled them at her. "Nothing! I do not believe it. Here—" I held the book closer. "Look again," I said. "Touch the page."

She hesitated.

"It is okay. I will help you." I took her slender hand, pressed her fingers to the empty parchment.

She gasped, eyes widening in wonder.

"Do you see it now?"

She nodded, innocent eagerness spreading upon her face. She giggled, pushing her hand against the page. "It tickles."

I smiled, watched as threads of ebony smoke snaked upward, wrapping tender fingers about her wrists. She shivered, puffed a breathy sigh, leaned forward, eyes intent as the sooty strands wound smoldering ribbons up her arms, teasing her flesh. They paused at her eyes, gathering into a bouquet of sable roses, quivering in the dimming light.

Her delight grew. "They're wonderful," she gasped.

"They are," I said as the wispy coils shot into her eyes.

She convulsed for an instant, her mouth pursing into an astonished exclamation before her face slackened and her lithe body relaxed. The life glimmering in her eyes faded and those elfin orbs sank back into her skull, void and empty.

Diminutive flames flickered across the surface of the vellum, etching a portrait of Hollie Daugherty on the page. They winked out moments later. In their place, stared her smiling, joyful visage, her eyes agleam with life and blessed innocence.

As I watched, fingers of golden fire etched her name into the bottom of her page with a grand flourish. I closed the book and dropped it into a pocket before carefully and reverently laying her body beside her mother's.

Emerson Daugherty

"Hey, Emmie. What ya doing?"

A slimy mist crushed me with cold, brittle hands, leprous white fingers that caressed my body in ways that made me shudder. I tried to hug myself but couldn't find my arms.

"It's a trip, isn't it?"

"Who are you?"

A malevolent chuckle. "Who do you think I am?"

A sudden flash of lightning. Colors whirling, smearing into themselves, creating a kaleidoscope of insanity. I squeezed my eyes closed. "Make it stop."

The reeling carousel stuttered to a stop, threw me from where I stood into an acid-trip void. Gaudy wooden horses ogled, gaped, and glowered, lancing my mind with psychedelic shades. The pigments splashed and splattered across a quavery canvas.

I screamed.

Daisy Pellerman glared at me from my bedroom doorway, her patterned, pastel-pink cotton nightgown drenched with scarlet, dripping goo onto the floor at her shriveled feet. She wiped her nose with a bloody wrist, smeared crimson across her lip. Her other hand gripped a revolver, tapping the barrel against her hip. Tap. Tap. Tap.

She smiled, the corners of her lips slashed, blood oozing from the wounds dribbling down her chin. "It's all your fault, you know. That we're dead."

I shook my head, staring, mouth trembling, stomach knotted. "I didn't mean to look at my mommy's pictures," I said. "I didn't know that my daddy would get so mad. Please—"

"Too late," she snapped. "Too late for apologies. Too late for forgiveness. Too late for your daddy. Too late for your mommy."

The pitch of her voice rose to a lyrical, sing-song tone that grated down my spine.

"You weren't his, you know."

I shook my head, yanked my knees to my chest, hugged my legs, scraped my bare feet against the floor, trying to pass through the wall, to escape, wake up, anything that would pull me from this nightmare.

"Please," I whimpered. "Make it stop."

"I'm a whore. You're a whore. Everyone's a whore, whore." A pause. "You know," she said. "That old McDonald fella didn't run a very tight ship." She stepped into my room, pressed the muzzle of the gun against the side of her head. "Hey," she said. "Wanna see brains come out of my mouth?" She opened her mouth, dislocating her jaw to create a gaping cavern.

She pulled the trigger.

Emptiness.

A man, broad-shouldered with thick arms and powerful hands, knelt beside me, wearing compassion on his face. He lifted my chin so that I would look at him. Recognition sloshed through my sluggish brain. "Mommy's friend," I breathed into the silence.

"More than that. Much more."

A breath of icy wind grazed my cheek. A likeness wavered, the face stepping into and out of focus. My face, yet masculine, sharp-angled and hawkish, pine-green eyes that seared holes through the soul. Lips sheared from granite yanked into a sneer, the knife-edged corners touching luminous eyes dripping with rancor and spite.

The flickering lights pulsed.

"You see it. I know you see it." An unhinged giggle rattled the air. "That's what I wanted. For you to know me."

My eyes widened. Perception chipped jagged holes through my denial. Recognition welled, drowned me in the realization of who I was.

I shook my head. "No. No. No. You can't be...You're not—"

Dismay dogged my denial. The smirk faltered.

The vacillating face dissolved. "If you want to know the truth, come for your daughter. You know where. He'll be waiting."

Desolation. Blankness. Abandonment.

Sudden explosive brightness.

I screamed. "Maggie!"

Hands pushed me down, crushed me beneath insistent and desperate pressure. I thrashed. Searing agony stabbed and sliced through my shoulder and knee. Desperate voices shouted.

My hand found a metal pole.

I yanked it, smacked it into a hovering body.

A grunt. The body staggered back. The hands holding me down vanished.

I jerked my other hand. Steel bit into my wrist, cold, ragged teeth sawing through flesh.

"Where the hell is my daughter?"

"Hold her down, damn it. You, get her head, hold it still before she tears something else. You, you, and you, arms and legs. Watch that damned knee. Get her IV under control.

"What the hell is going on in here?"

My head bucked up on a doddering neck, eyes clawing at a dim, hazy form dressed in a black uniform, gun belt, pistol hugging a broad hip. My strength failed.

A biting chill strolled up my arm, spread into my shoulder and chest.

My flailing waned. Oblivion gouged the light from my mind. Joyless, grief-stricken fingers warped into meat hooks. They grabbed flesh and muscle, dragged me screaming into the darkness.

Daniel (Danni) McMillan

Danni pulled his cruiser to the curb one house up from Micah Griffith's single-story brick ranch, killed the headlights, left the engine running for the heat.

A light snow swirled through the darkness. The eye of the storm that had dumped twenty-four inches in the mountains surrounding Ruby Creek in less than twelve hours, closing the two-lane highways into and out of town, sealing them away from the rest of the world. And, if you believed the weather reports, they were expecting another thirty-six to forty-eight inches over the next two days.

Danni didn't believe the weather reports. They were always light on the expected accumulation.

The wipers slapped the edges of the windshield, the cadence matching the beat of his thumping heart. He peered into the nearly snow-blind night. Micah's cruiser hunkered in the driveway, snow drifting against the tires and piling over the roof, trunk, and hood.

The house glared at him, sullen and cheerless, the windows curtained and dark.

He thought about calling Micah's cell again. His gut roiled, spitted, and turned slowly over glowing coals. Why the hell did he agree to this posting? It wouldn't lead anywhere. But that never mattered. It's just what you did if you were a McMillan in Ruby Creek. Everything for family. Nothing for yourself.

At least that's what he told himself every time an opportunity came up for him to get out.

And now Emmie had come back. For Daisy's funeral and to support Sam through his grief. But there'd been something else. He saw it in her eyes when she lied about when she was leaving. Something that had to do with the desecration of Daisy's corpse and Sam's murder. And despite the evidence, he refused to believe that Emmie had done what it looked like she had done.

Nothing made any sense.

Gale Henderson's voice chimed through the back of his thoughts, his explanation gouging chunks from Danni's disbelief.

He glanced at the journal he'd discovered in Emmie's SUV. Dread constricted his chest.

"Dispatch. This is unit one."

Static crackled over the radio.

"Go ahead, Danni."

"I'm at Micah's. His cruiser is parked in the drive. Snowbound. No visible activity inside the house." He paused, peered through the snowfall, dread snailing across his mind. "I'm going to see if anyone's home."

"You want backup?"

He bit his lip. Was there anyone left to send as backup?

"Negative," he said. "Standby."

Rice crispies snapped, crackled, and popped through the connection for an instant before blessed quiet.

Pulling a steadying breath, Danni exited his cruiser and trudged the thirty yards through the ice-aged tundra to the porch, stomping snow and ice from his shoes, and shaking the kitchen freezer from his shoulders. His finger hesitated against the doorbell, a niggling thought teasing the back of his brain. He tried the doorknob instead.

It turned, squeaked grudgingly in the cold as he pushed the door open and stepped through, stuttered back a step, assaulted by the reek of blood, urine, and feces.

Trying not to hyperventilate, Danni slipped inside and caught his breath. Service weapon in hand, he snapped his flashlight on, swept the entry with the light, snapped it off. Spring-coiled quiet stood beside him.

The frigid wind buffeted him from behind, ice-tinged fingers tossing snowflakes into his hair and down the neck of his jacket and shirt, urging him forward. Danni stepped onto the landing, swallowed down the apprehension stuffing cotton down his throat.

"Micah?" he called. "It's Danni." The lump in his throat bobbed. The house creaked and groaned in response. His dread grew. He snapped the flashlight on again, stepped from the entry into the family room, turned left, stumbled back into the wall, almost dropping the flashlight.

He clamped his mouth shut on a scream. His hand trembled, bouncing the flashlight beam off the carnage.

"Shit. Shit. Shit."

Micah leaned against the wall to his left, chest sunken, face gaunt and hollow, his dead eyes empty and staring nowhere. Micah's wife, Linda, slouched against the opposite wall, the Berber carpet below her soaked lobster red. A scarlet hole gaped from her left eye, and a crimson, postmodern painting splattered the ivory wall behind her head. A third body lay on its side beside her, back pressed into the wall, head touching Linda's thigh. A man. Vaguely familiar, the top of his skull missing, bone, brain and hair were smeared across the carpet like jigsaw puzzle pieces shaken and tossed from the box.

The fourth body sat piled into itself near the center of the room, eyeing Linda, a pistol clutched in the left hand. Danni couldn't see the face, but the ragged cut of the hair, dyed raven black and shot through with violet and rust red streaks, the spindly arms, stooped shoulders, and bony, angular body told Danni what he wanted to know. Anthony, Micah, and Linda's oldest child and only son.

Danni's knees smacked the floor. He bent over and vomited.

He reached for his radio, hesitated. Where was their daughter, Paige? He peered through the shadows, hugging the hallway to the back of the house. Gritting his teeth, he shoved himself to his feet, muttering to himself. He blew out a hushed breath, turned off his flashlight, stepped into the corridor.

Dusky light seeped from beneath a closed door on the left. Danni padded toward it, back scuffing the opposite wall, trying to recall if that room belonged to Paige.

He pressed his ear to the door. Breathless silence wriggled through the paper-thin hollow-core plywood.

He shouldered through the door.

Gangly plywood splintered. The lock exploded, metal pieces clattering to the floor as the door burst inward, spraying shattered wood, a hinge tearing from the frame.

From a step inside, Danni aimed his pistol and swept his flashlight through the gloom. The beam settled on the twin bed in the center of the room. Paige sprawled on top, eyes staring upward, skin sallow and shrunken.

"Paige?" Danni stepped to the side of the bed, trepidation wrangling his gut. He reached out, hesitated, fist clenched in indecision. "Paige?"

No answer. No movement. No acknowledgment of his presence.

She stared into nothing, red-webbed eyes blank, flesh pale, jaw drooping open. Beside her head lay a piece of paper, a page torn from a book, a threadbare and frayed outline on the smudged surface. Danni picked it up and gasped. He turned his gaze back to Paige, shook his head.

"It's not possible," he mumbled.

At the creak of wood behind him, Danni spun around. He staggered back into the wall beside the bed, pistol raised, weaving drunkenly, the beam from the flashlight bouncing off the floor, ceiling, and walls.

"What the hell?" he said, his voice rising an octave, tone incredulous.

Micah stood in the doorway. "Hello, Danni boy. How the hell have you been?"

Danni shook his head, wiped sweat from his brow, the gun trembling in his hand. "You're dead."

Micah shrugged. "Yeah, well. What can a corpse say to that?" He stepped into the room.

Danni pressed himself against the wall. "Don't."

Hands rose in supplication, the skin waxen, beginning to slough from the bone. "Going to shoot a dead guy?" The start of a cadaverous grin stretched the ends of his lips. The skin tightened and tore. "That's gotta be bad form in any universe."

Still shaking his head, Danni scooted to his right, away from the bed, toward the corner of the room, attempting to add distance between him and Micah's body.

Cataract-clouded eyes tracked him, the void behind the sockets peering at him with curiosity. "Just got a message to deliver. And then you can shoot me or do whatever the hell you want. Though, if I have a say, I'd rather not have any more holes punched through me." He lifted his uniform shirt, displayed the bloody gash goring his side below his ribs. "See what I mean?" He dropped the tail of his shirt. "Anyway, you and a plus one are invited to an exclusive affair to be held this evening at the old Daugherty estate. You know the one. It's been the talk of the town for twenty years." He winked, the motion stretching his pallid flesh. "Midnight, sharp." Micah stumbled back from the doorway, body swaying on suddenly rubbery legs. "Oh yeah. Your plus one needs to be Emerson Daugherty. And don't be late. Fashionable or not, it's just rude."

Micah collapsed.

Danni lowered his weapon and stared, heart hammering in his chest.

The Quixote

I STOOD BACK WITHIN the embrace of the winter eve's shadows, cloaked in my leather duster and fedora. I pulled a drag from the Camel clenched between my teeth, the incandescent orange glow illuminating my face. After holding the acidic smoke in my chest for two languid heartbeats, I blew it out through my nose. The frigid draft skulking through the ruins of the abandoned Daugherty estate teased the blue-white haze, tossing the trembling threads between the ragged cracks and seams gouging the decaying walls.

Fresh snow littered the debris scattered about the fractured and splintered elm flooring, the once burnished glow lackluster and colorless. The air stank of frigid arctic nothingness, the scents and smells imprisoned behind bars of ice and ruthless cold.

A plaintive sob snagged my attention. Memories of another such cry scratched at the chains shackling my guilt.

My little Dulcinea huddled into herself, scrunched into a tiny hole deep within a tattered mountain of smashed and riven wood furniture, swaddled in a pastel pink and white crocheted blanket I'd secured from Samuel's domicile, despite the heat wafting toward her from a propane camping tent heater. It glowed orange-red in the pitch-black, its shimmering beacon illuminating her fearful countenance.

"I want my mommy."

I jerked an ephemeral smile, crushed the Camel beneath the toe of my boot, and strode from the shadows. Dulcinea puffed a hushed gasp, shrank back, squeezed her legs tighter into her body, dug her chin into the tip of her chest. Her frightened, distrustful gaze hammered me, her slender mouth turned downward into a suspicious frown.

My smile deepened. "Dulcinea," I said. "My beloved child."

"My name's Maggie," she corrected. "And I'm not allowed to talk to strangers."

"Of course." I knelt beside her, reached to smooth a patch of tangled hair from her porcelain-delicate face. She shied from my touch, covered her head with the blanket, her boots scraping the warped and splintered wood as she tried to push herself deeper into her tiny cavern.

I lifted the blanket, stroked the top of her head, smoothing back her unruly curls. She flinched, shrunk deeper into herself.

"Go away."

I sighed, sat cross-legged, pretended to warm my hands within the gentle glow of the heater. "My dear, dear Dulcinea," I said, my tone tender and understanding. "I am not a stranger. Your mommy and I have known one another since—" I paused, staring into the fathomless depths of long-ago memories. "Since she was your age. I shall not harm you. I want only to...love and protect you. Forever. Which I promise. Upon my life."

"I want my mommy."

"And she shall be here," I said. "I have messengers delivering invitations to our intimate gathering as we speak."

"Promise?"

"I would not lie to you, my beloved."

The blanket slid below her eyes. She stared, distrust and indecision hovering in her gaze. "Pinky swear?"

I pouted my lower lip. "I do not know what that is, but if it is important to you, then yes, I shall pinky swear."

She jutted out a fist from the cramped confines of the blanket, curled pinky extended in invitation. I hesitated, uncertain of what I should do next. She shoved it toward me with impatience. "C'mon," she said. "You promised."

Still unsure, I extended my gloved hand, winced when my blood-stained finger hooked hers. She shook it firmly and released my hand, sneaking hers back behind the armor of her blanket.

"When will my mommy be here?" she asked, her voice shivering with doubt.

"Soon," I said. "And she is bringing another friend."

"Another friend?" She sat up, her covering sliding down past her chest. She clutched it to her stomach, unexpected excitement dancing from her eyes. She squinted, frowning with intense concentration. Seconds later, her face beamed with childish delight. "The policeman from the hotel! I like him!"

I nodded sagely, "As do I," I said, and winked. "He is a wonderful friend, indeed. An old one, and fondly remembered by your momma, despite what she might say. But perhaps not as old or cherished a friend as I." I deposited my book in my lap, opened the cover, antique leather groaning into the quiet.

My Dulcinea straightened, craned her neck to gain a better view. "What's that?"

I indulged her with a friendly smile. "A story book," I said. "An antique and precious story book. It's been in my family for...oh, since before I can remember." I opened the pages, their parched edges rustling as I turned them. "Does your momma read to you?"

"Sometimes. But just little kid stories."

"Tell me."

She made a face, eyes squinting, as she thought. "I don't know," she said. "Stuff like *Bambi*, *The Little Mermaid*, *Tangled*, *Lady and the Tramp*. You know, little kid stories."

"Ah, I see." I paused and gazed down at the book, the parchment quivering in keen eagerness. "Would you like me to read you a story while we wait for your momma and her policeman friend?"

"What kind of story?"

"Oh, the best kind of story ever. Filled with knights in shining armor, damsels in distress, villains, and of course, dragons." I winked at her.

"What's a damsel?"

"A kind and gentle lady like yourself."

She huffed. "I'm not a damsel."

"Well," I said, smoothing a page, "why don't we read the story and when we're done, you can tell me if you think you're a damsel or not."

"Okay." She settled back, hands clenched between her knees above the blanket, enthusiasm glowing from her face.

I read from my book, the words flowing gently from the pages.

The frozen air quivered between us. She sighed, settled back, her expression dreamy, and gaze whimsical, an ethereal smile spreading over her lips. I paused.

"Don't stop, Pappa," she said, her voice breathy and heavy with encroaching slumber, her eyelids sinking downward. "Read to me about Don Quixote."

I smiled, turning the pages, and began reading to my little dove.

Emerson Daugherty

WAS I AWAKE OR still unconscious, my mind wandering the universe in search of sanity?

Pain throbbed everywhere, punched my ribs every time I breathed. My arm and shoulder argued, their vehement disagreement pounding my head. My knee joined the discordant chorus, chiming in every few heartbeats, its vocalizations sharp and stinging, the opinions it uttered dripping with outrage.

I moaned, opened my eyes.

Softened shadows strolled the edges of my hospital room, clutched the eaves where the tiled ceiling met the pastel orange colors splashed across the walls. Muted, inset lights bathed the air above me in a delicate and mellow shroud, promising rest and an easy, dreamless sleep.

Liars, all of them.

The room stank of antiseptic, sweat, and urine. I wrinkled my nose in disgust, tried to lift my right arm to wipe the snot from my top lip. My shoulder screeched at me, stabbing spikes down my arm. Blinking the tears from my eyes, I peered to my left, rattled the leather restraint binding my left arm.

Well, ain't this cozy?

Why was I restrained?

Hazy and indistinct memories scurried through the detritus littering my thoughts.

Daisy slouched in a dining room chair, empty sockets glued to me, her slack mouth muttering "Whore, whore, whore."

Sam knelt beside her, squeezing her hand, a hysterical sneer riding his lips as he goaded her.

Sam's service pistol swam across the floor toward me, bumped into my left hand. Outrage and bitterness sank fangs into my neck. I screamed, snatched up Sam's gun, pulled the trigger. Daisy's body jerked twice, slithered from the chair, plopping bonelessly on the floor. Sam stared, scarlet blossoming beneath his shirt. He toppled over, glaring accusation and indictment at me.

Carnage and blood, rollicking with deranged giggles.

My eyes opened. My body raged. My chest heaved.

Multicolored lights skated across a monitor, mated numbers bouncing and beeping.

My door whooshed open. A nurse bulled through, stalled just inside the threshold. "What the hell?" he said. "She's coding. Get the doc in here. Now!" He rushed to my bedside, slapped a blue button on the wall above me.

Blue lights convulsed, bayoneting me with the razor sharpened end of a whittled stick.

Sadistic chortling.

A wraithlike, ghastly body stood over me, sniggering.

My body bucked and bounced.

The pulsating lights evaporated. Blackness swooped in, seizing me in a subzero embrace. The frenzied shouts ricocheting past me snuffed out. Dead-air stomped through the vacuum, squatted and stared.

A familiar face floated into view, blank eyes dripping acid, burning smoking holes into my flesh.

"Sorry, baby girl," he said. "Can't die yet. Not allowed. Not until it's finished, and he has what he came back for." A sudden theatrical pause. "You know, I almost feel sorry for you. Almost wish I could have you back. We'd make a hell of a team." A wink. "Almost."

"Maggie?" I whispered.

Hysterical chuckles. The shake of a shaggy head. An eyeball sagged from its ramshackle socket. A decomposing hand shoved it back. "Already spoken for, my love."

A face came close, falling apart at the seams, the stench of rancid breath washing over my face.

I gagged.

"Should've done better keeping that sprite safe, little darling." A thoughtful expression creased the leprous brow, the decomposing hand rubbing the skeletal chin as the dead, smoldering eyes looked up into the darkness. "Come to think of it, baby girl, maybe you should've listened to your gut seven years ago in Denver, and not whored yourself out to that no good bamboozling snake." The unsympathetic gaze swiveled down. "Of course, if you hadn't gotten wasted that night...we wouldn't be here now, would we?" The face contorted into a puzzled expression. "I am a little confused. Why would you come back to help bury the one woman in all of Ruby Creek who despised and treated you like crap?" A breathy silence.

"I didn't come back to bury her."

The face lifted. "Ah." An eye winked. A low throated and callous chuckle ping-ponged my brain. "I see. Too bad ol' Sammy Pellerman didn't prepare you better for what was coming. Instead, just fattened the calf for its sacrifice."

My body bucked. Electricity jolted my lurching heart.

"You're my mommy's friend. The one in her pictures."

Surprise. And hesitation.

"You're my dad."

The mangled face drew close, dead eyes flaring, rotted lips pinched. "Hope you're not expecting a Star Wars moment, little princess."

"Help me destroy him. Please."

Ice melted, refroze.

"Can't. Sorry to disappoint."

Skeleton fingers splayed against my thumping chest. "Anyhoo, been a blast getting acquainted. Too bad we couldn't have done it for reals."

An icy hand reached into my body, pricked my stuttering heart with a moldering fingertip.

My eyes fluttered open. Unfocused reality huddled beside me. Quiet, rhythmic beeps nudged me, tried to convince me that everything was okay. I was alive. And that was the only thing that mattered.

Only, it wasn't.

The Tall Man had my Maggie. And I needed to get her back from the bastard before I sent his rotting corpse back to hell. Whatever it took.

The scrape of denim against cheap orange vinyl snatched my attention.

"About damn time."

A familiar voice from the shadows.

The rustle of hushed footsteps approaching. A face emerging from the darkness, unshaven and haggard, gaunt, eyes bruised and sleep deprived. Mouth pinched into a tight, straight line, his expression sorrowful and brimming with indecision.

"You still alive?"

I stared, my jaw working as I chewed the memory of my near-death experience.

Had it been real or imagined? I didn't see the bright light. I didn't see my body from above as the doctors and nurses worked to make my heart work again. I'd only seen a nightmare hosted by a ghoul I knew to be my biological dad. My mom's special friend, the one in the pictures with her. The one that had precipitated my parents' argument and their eventual murder and suicide.

But he had saved me from the Tall Man, the Quixote, before he could take my soul.

And had paid a terrible price for his interference.

If there was a Quixote, there was also a Sancho.

And it had been Sancho, not my dad, that had cannoned me from death.

My stomach churned. I clenched my teeth, stomped down on the bile as it bubbled from the back of my throat.

Danni stared, indecision and disbelief gurgling behind his eyes. Would he believe me when I told him that the Ruby Creek curse was real? I wasn't religious, but I said a small, quick prayer. I didn't have time for anything else.

I rattled the leather restraint with a liquid wrist. "I need to get out of here," I said, my voice weak and thin. "He's got Maggie. He's going to kill her."

A furrowed brow. "Who has Maggie?"

Screw sanity. "The Tall Man has her."

"The Tall who?" He eyeballed me with disbelief.

"You won't believe me," I said. "I wouldn't believe me."

"Try me."

Sandpaper scraped my throat raw. "The Quixote."

An indication of an indulgent smile. "You're right, I don't believe you." Six quick strides to his chair and back. He tossed a book at me. "Is that why you have this?"

I lifted my head. Tristan Daugherty's journal glowered at me. "Yes. Sam—"

"Gave it to you. Yeah, I figured. I read through it. Pretty heady stuff. A bit looney tunes for my taste, but an interesting read."

"You have to believe me," I said.

Pinched lips. Sudden flaring rage banked as quickly as it flashed. "I don't have to do anything," he said. "Did you steal Daisy's corpse from the funeral home? Did you murder Sam? Did you—"

Dingy memories paraded through my mind. Daisy and Sam. Together and dead. "I don't—"

He gripped the bed railing, knuckles bulging white in the subdued light. "Don't bullshit me, Emmie. The responding unit discovered you sprawled over Sam's body, Daisy's corpse spread-eagled next to him, bullet holes in both their chests, Sam's service weapon in your hand." He stopped, spittle dripping from his mouth. He wiped it clean. "Should I continue?"

"No."

"Aren't you going to protest your innocence now? Tell me that the Quixote made you do it, that you didn't have a choice?" His voice rose an octave with each word until he shrilled like a hysterical toddler.

"No," I said. "I'm not going to protest my innocence, because I shot Daisy's body. And I shot Sam. But he was already dead."

He shook his head so hard I thought he'd break his neck.

"And I didn't have a choice," I said. "Because the Quixote doesn't leave room for denials. His victims aren't random. He selects them for very specific reasons and then carries out his honorable justice. Judge. Jury. Executioner."

"Like your parents?"

A twisted knife through the heart. I blanched, looked away.

"Convenient," he said. "But not a practical defense strategy."

I nudged at Daugherty's journal with my chin. "You read Tristan Daugherty's journal. You tell me."

A derisive snort. "A familial curse," he said. "Enacted on the members of the four Ruby Creek founding families once every generation. By a man swearing justice for the murders of his wife, daughter, and himself."

I met his glare.

"More bullshit."

"Daugherty. McMillan. Pellerman. Barrett," I said. "Each founding family line. Each generation. On or around December twenty-one."

He looked away.

"Who else has died over the past twenty-four hours?" I asked.

His face paled.

I'd cracked his armor, driven the tip of the spear through. He pretended I hadn't.

Uneasiness. A hard swallow. His mouth opened, closed. Skepticism. Then, "Bobby and Becky Barrett and their daughter, Gracie," he began, his voice shaking. "Sam—"

"Pellerman," I interrupted.

He cleared his throat, looked at me.

"Who else?"

"I found Micah Griffith and his family dead in their home before coming here." Tears welled in his eyes, dripped down his face. "Paige was in her bed, a pillow under her head. She looked like she was sleeping, except for the hemorrhages in her eyes."

"Griffith?"

"Second or third McMillan cousins from Linda's side."

"That leaves a Daugherty family member," I said. "Which means I don't have much time. Once he has a Daugherty, he'll take Maggie."

"Why Maggie?"

"For the one that got away twenty years ago."

His face reddened.

"Let me go," I said. "You can tell your men and the mayor that I overpowered you. I'll even shoot you. For more realism."

"They won't buy it."

"So you believe me now."

"I don't know what to believe," he said.

He caught me staring, looked away.

"There's something else," I said.

"No."

"You were a terrible liar in high school. You're worse now," I said.

He gripped the bed rail, sucked down a quivering breath. "After I found Paige, Micah's corpse visited me in her room." He wiped his brow with a shaking hand. "He...it invited me and a plus one to an intimate soirée being held at your old childhood home at midnight. Micah suggested I bring you as my plus one."

Chills skipped down my body, chased the sweat clinging to my hospital gown.

"You can't ignore that summons," I said.

"Why not?"

"Because the Quixote wants me as well as Maggie. If we don't show, he'll take Maggie and then he'll kill someone else from your family line just to watch you squirm. You'll be marked for life. Like me."

"I don't understand."

Still not the sharpest tool in the shed.

"I'm not a biological Daugherty," I said. "Deacon Barrett was my dad."

Doubt flashed from his eyes. "How—?"

"Trust me, I just know."

"Then I'll go. Alone."

"You'll be dead," I said. "Probably the Quixote's new Sancho, and he'll still have Maggie."

Danni ran a hand through his hair.

I rattled the restraint. "I came back to end it," I said. "Help me do that. And get my daughter back."

Daniel (Danni) McMillan

SNOW PELTED THE WINDSHIELD of Danni's cruiser, the quarter-sized flakes splattering against the glass, the wipers working frantically to clear the violence. He glanced at Emmie in the passenger seat; her face highlighted in the dusky amber glow from the dash lights, gaze turned toward the journal in her lap.

The hulking silhouette of her old childhood home, abandoned after the murder and suicide of her parents, glowered, shaking a defiant fist at the faux moonlight glinting off the wintry storm. Dim light flickered from an upstairs window, tossing yellow-black fragments through the grimed glass. A gloomy silhouette fouled the haggard curtain draped over the window. It hovered for an instant, then vanished.

Dread crouched on Danni's shoulder, whispered death into his ear.

"How did you survive the first time?"

Emmie handed him a frayed and creased page torn from a book. He unfolded it, stared at the shapeless outline of a young girl's face, kinked hair scrabbling over her shoulders, with bright, incandescent eyes, puckish nose, and an impish mouth.

"I tore that from his book before he could consummate his curse."

Danni frowned, handed back the page. "But how?"

She shrugged. "My dad interrupted him in the middle of the story. The Quixote didn't have time to finish it." She leaned forward, peered through the frosting glass. "He knows we're here," she said. "He's waiting for us."

Danni swallowed down the stone squatting in his throat. "I'm going to die, aren't I?"

Emmie smiled, leaned over and brushed her lips across his cheek. "Not on my watch, mister." She draped her coat across her right shoulder, snugged it closed. "I get the shotgun," she said.

"I don't think so, dude." Danni nodded at her right arm, immobilized in a black shoulder sling. "You can't even move that thing."

"I've had worse."

"I don't think so. Here." He handed her his service pistol and two extra magazines. "Fifteen plus one in the chamber. Can you load and rack with one hand?"

"Does a bear—"

"Yeah, great." He helped her dump the magazines into her left coat pocket. "Locked and loaded. Make them count."

"Remember," she said. "It's all about the book. Destroy that and we destroy him."

"Easy peasy lemon squeezy," he said.

"I always hated that phrase." Emmie opened her door and stumbled into the teeth of the stormy, snow-laced wind.

Danni shuddered, snugged his gloves, shouldered his door open. The hinges moaned, the sound echoing off the scraggly ponderosa and pinon pine, scrambling blindly along each side of the drive.

Moving slowly to accommodate Emmie's stiff limp, shotgun pressed into his shoulder, he trudged the few yards to the dilapidated cedar deck, the once pristine wood cracked, broken, and splintered.

The steps buckled beneath their weight, the cadaverous planks cracking with each careful step.

He lingered at the front door, grasped the knob with a trembling fist, resisted the urge to drape his finger over the shotgun trigger. He touched his ear to the coarse, craggy wood, listened, thought he heard...what?

Music?

Dread threw him to the wolves.

He pushed open the door. The rusted hinges moaned, froze when the door opened a few inches. Danni licked panic-desiccated lips, glanced back at Emmie. She huddled against the disintegrating wall left of the door, his pistol gripped in her left hand. It trembled.

"You ready?" he whispered.

She nodded.

He pushed through the doorway. Emmie followed, her right foot scraping the debris-littered floor.

The blackened outlines of jumbled furniture and garbage glowered from the darkness. He flicked on the light mounted to the shotgun, swept the entry and the living room, sucked in an abrupt breath.

"Shit," Emmie whispered beside him.

Three bodies huddled affectionately around a propane tent heater, bathed in an inviting orange-yellow glow that emphasized the savage wounds gouged into faces and heads, eyes clouded and vacant, their bloodless flesh beginning to darken at the edges.

Except for the girl.

Emmie sucked in a panicked breath.

Maybe five or six. She leaned back against a shattered table, limp hair luminous, small, empty eyes dancing with delight, her mouth turned up into a contented and joyful smile.

Emmie staggered past him, touched the girl with trembling fingers, breathed relief, her shoulders slumping. She turned, shook her head.

The blood drained from Danni's face. He shuddered and shrank back.

Russell and Lacey Daugherty. Their daughter Hollie.

Daugherty. McMillan. Pellerman. Barrett.

What the hell was he doing here? Why hadn't he called for backup? Because he wasn't supposed to be here. And no one was coming to bail his sorry ass out of this hot water.

The shuffling scrape of leather across shattered and rotting wood.

"Emmie?" He turned, found emptiness. "Emmie!" He swept the sudden vacuum with his light, heard the distant sounds of thump, scrape, grunt from the stairway, stabbed the light in that direction, painted Emmie's back as she struggled up the stairs, one painful, creaking step at a time. "Emmie!" He stumbled over his pistol.

A hushed, melodious voice skipped down the stairs, wound a delightful sing-song tune around his mind, plucking his thoughts with shrill, off-key notes. Danni staggered, nearly dropped the shotgun as screaming meemies rollicked through his gut.

Emmie vanished at the top of the stairs.

Muttering curses, Danni vaulted after her, wood groaning with each pounding step, his curses reverberating off the sagging walls and ceiling. He hesitated at the top, swept the hall with his flashlight, clicked it off when the beam touched a guttering light dancing along the bottom of the first door on his right.

He didn't see Emmie.

The singing grew louder, the words indistinct and nonsensical.

The made-up song of a young child.

Danni swallowed down the terror scraping the back of his throat, stepped onto the landing.

The singing stopped.

The bedroom door creaked open, dumping pallid yellow light across the floor. A rotted outline stretched from the room, tapped the opposite wall, molded itself into the emaciated figure of a tall, corpse-like man cloaked and shrouded in an unnatural blackness.

Danni hugged the wall, hesitated at the edge of the light knifing past him. A shrill, hysterical giggle from inside the room pulled at his mind. He rounded the corner, shotgun aimed.

"It's Danni, the policeman!" a young girl's high-pitched voice screeched with delight. "My momma's pimp boyfriend from high school!"

Danni lowered the shotgun and gaped at the young girl sitting on the deteriorated and shabby bed, sheets and bedspread molding and rancid, the fabric torn and tattered.

"Maggie?"

She snickered. "No, silly beans. My name is Dulcinea."

Emmie lay beside her, eyes blank and staring.

"Hello, Daniel."

Danni spun to his left, raising the shotgun, and faced the owner of the cadaverous shadow welling into the hallway.

Needle-thin, bloodless lips stretched over an uneven row of sickly yellow and blackened teeth into a horrific smile, chilling Danni to his soul.

"I have been expecting you," he said. "Though you and your erstwhile high school sweetheart are unfashionably early." The Quixote's expression darkened. "A disheartening turn of events." He looked at Maggie. "Tell me, my little dove, what shall we do with him while we wait for your momma to arrive?"

Danni fired the shotgun.

Emerson Daugherty

FLASHING IMAGES ROLLICKING THROUGH my thoughts. Voices whispering words. A little girl's giggles. The soothing caress of a gentle and loving voice.

I sat in my rocking chair beside the fire, my sewing crumpled and forgotten between my hands as I listened to Francisco read from the tales of Don Quixote to our precious Dulcinea. A burning log cracked, spitting a storm of sparks from the hearth. They scattered against the packed dirt floor, winking out in a breath. I closed my eyes, breathed in the earthy smell as it mingled with the scents of cedar and pine, two of my favorites. I breathed out, letting loose the tension and anxiety clinging to my body.

Dulcinea giggled, asked a whispered question of her pappa. Francisco answered, his tone serious yet gentle. I smiled at his fondness for our daughter, wondered again what his reaction would be to my news.

I touched my hands to my stomach, allowed a satisfied smile to slide over my face. It had been four years of trying. Two miscarriages that broke our hearts if not our spirits. And now, the blessed La Virgen María had heard and granted my most ardent prayer.

Francisco emerged from Dulcinea's corner, a lopsided grin upon his face.

"I am sorry for ignoring you, my darling. But I cannot refuse a request to read *Don Quixote* to our dear Dulcinea."

He sat beside me, kissed my cheek.

"Apology accepted."

Golden firelight danced through his salt-and-pepper-streaked hair.

"Is she asleep?"

"Yes, my love."

"You indulge the child too much."

"How can I not?" he said. "She is our only one."

I set down my sewing, took his hand, and placed it over my stomach. "Not for much longer."

He gaped in astonishment. "Truly?" he said.

I nodded, cupped his chin in my hand, and kissed his lips. "Yes, my love. La Virgen María has granted our prayers and blessed us with a second child. The little one shall join our family in seven months."

"Hello, princess."

The scenery wavered for an instant, dissolved into a gray mist, and vanished.

"Where—?"

"A magnificent story. Except, it isn't yours."

I looked up into the deep shadows clinging to the drooping ceiling, which hung over the sagging, moldering bed on which I lay. Lantern light cast an uncertain glow through a dank and rotting room. A child sat next to me, her knees pulled to her chest, slender arms hugging her legs. She stared at me, her expression corkscrewed into suspicious indecision.

Lancing pain sliced through my right side and throbbed through my knee.

Get up!

The command startled me. Yet my mind remained disconnected from my body.

"Who are you?"

"You already know."

"Come out where I can see you."

"Sorry, buttercup. This is the best you're going to get. If he knew I was here—"

My skull throbbed. My chest heaved, but my body wouldn't respond to my brain's desperate commands.

"I need to you to wake up." A quiet, hysterical snicker. Angry words muttered in response. "I need you to step out of the story."

"What story?"

"His story."

"Why?"

"Because it isn't your story."

Gunshots shattered the silence. Horses screamed. Men shouted. Glass shattered. Flames sprouted from the floor, crawled up the walls, hugged the ceiling, flung black, stinging smoke.

"Momma!"

"Dulcinea!" I rolled to my stomach, spat blood and goo, my chest shattered.

"Maggie." The name uttered from far off, barely heard.

"Francisco!"

"Is dead."

"No," I screamed.

"Has been for one hundred thirty years."

"Momma."

I reached into the smoke, coughed. "Dulcinea!"

"Maggie!" The name louder, the voice more insistent and compelling.

Hurried footsteps slapped the wood floor. A dirty, foul-smelling shape shadowed me. A hand reached down, yanked me up by my collar, flung me through a gaping void.

"Wake up!"

I sat up.

Sweat drenched my hair and face, drooled down the sides of my head, soaking a decaying bedspread. Stale air quivered around me. Sour yellow light blinked from a guttering coal oil lamp, the faltering flame dull and lusterless.

A scratchy, sand-scraped voice read quietly from a book, wound wispy, snake-like tendrils through my jumbled thoughts.

The voice paused.

"Momma!"

"Maggie?" I reached out, grasped...emptiness. I swung my gaze around. Maggie snuggled in the Quixote's lap, encircled by his arm, his book resting on her small legs.

As my eyes found hers, she furrowed her brow and puckered her lips. "Who is Maggie?" she asked, looked into the glowering eyes above her. "Pappa, why does Mamma keep calling me Maggie?"

The Quixote smiled and lifted my daughter from his lap. He brushed the top of her head with a fatherly kiss that drove icy spear tips through my spine.

"She is confused, my dove," he said. "Her mind is contaminated by her...companion."

"I did not like him," Maggie said. "He was a nasty man."

The Quixote flashed an indulgent smile. "It is not polite to speak ill of the dead, my dove."

"The dead?"

A chagrined shrug. Chased by a cold, flat smile. "Daniel McMillan and the Daugherty family are enjoying one another's company in the great room downstairs," he said. "A spark may yet continue to breathe within him. I do not know. I do not care."

A lead weight crushed my heart.

Maggie looked over, swept me with a confused look before dropping her eyes in contrition. "I'm sorry, Pappa," she said. "I did not mean—"

"You are not to blame," he said, as he swung his gaze toward me. "Bad character corrupts good morals. Perhaps more time in our story will clear your momma's mind." He lifted his eyes to mine, the fond expression melting from his cadaverous face. "Or perhaps not." He touched Maggie's shoulder. "Please sit in your chair, my princess, and continue to read, so that Pappa and Momma may speak."

She hesitated, uncertainty stalking her eyes. "Yes, Pappa." She looked at me. "I hope you feel better soon, Momma."

She climbed into a decomposing rocker squatting in the far corner of the room, the paint faded and peeled, and buried herself in the book, her delicate lips moving in sync with the words caressing her mind.

I recognized that rocker. It had belonged to me.

"She is already mine," he said. "As you can see." A pause, his glowing eyes narrowing for a heartbeat. "I...we had hoped for you to join us in our story. To be a family again."

"She's my daughter, not yours," I said. "Your daughter is dead. And I am not your dear departed wife, Nayara. She's dead as well."

Animosity scorched the air between us. "As you say. No family is perfect, but I can offer you what this world cannot."

"Which is?"

"Eternal peace."

"No, thank you. I've experienced your eternal peace. I'd rather rot in hell."

"Your choice does not surprise me," he said. "But...I am disappointed that you shall not be joining Dulcinea and I—"

"Her name is Maggie."

A rueful smile tugged the corners of his emaciated lips. He rose, shrugged his shoulders into his leather duster, snugged his fedora onto his skeletal head. "My little dove and I shall miss her momma."

The bedroom door squealed open. Maggie looked up from the Quixote's book, curiosity perched on her face.

Daisy Pellerman's corpse shambled across the threshold, her dusty blue and faded violet floral print dress smeared with blood and mud. Two ragged holes glared from the center of her chest where I had shot her, the edges stained purple and red. The skin sagged from her skull, blackened with rot and decay, eyelids torn off, vacant eye sockets dripping a jaundiced yellow puss brimming with squirming maggots.

Maggie grinned, her eyes brightening with delight. She clapped her hands together. "It's Gramma Daisy," she said, turning her gaze toward me. "Look, Momma, it's Gramma Daisy. She's come to join our family. I wish Grampa Sam could join us, too."

"Dulcinea, my darling." The Quixote held out his hand to her.

Maggie jumped from the rocking chair, skipped into his waiting embrace, and handed him the book. He hugged her to his hip, pinned me with an exultant smile. "My dove, unfortunately, your momma has decided not to join our family. She would rather stay with...her friend."

The joy in Maggie's eyes withered. She looked up at the Quixote, her last sliver of hope burning to ash. She turned her gaze to me, sorrow and anger raging through her eyes. "Why, Momma?" she pleaded. "Why won't you join us?"

"Maggie," I said, my heart twisting in anguish.

Rage flashed. She stomped her foot. "My name is Dulcinea. Stop calling me Maggie!" She hugged the Quixote, her mouth twisted into a sulky pout. "I hate you," she said. "I hate you!" Tears streaming from her eyes, she bolted from the room and stomped down the stairs.

The Quixote sighed. "Unfortunate," he said. "But not unexpected." He looked at Daisy. "Please take Miss Daugherty to join her friend and the Daugherty family in the great room."

Daisy leered, her black hole eyes swiveling from me to the Quixote. "No." She raised her arm, her black rotting hand holding Danni McMillan's service weapon.

The Quixote arched a brow, slid a jackknife from inside his duster. "Interesting," he said, glancing at me. "Blood *is* thicker than water. It seems that your father has decided to do the 'right' thing." He turned his gaze back to Deacon Barrett's Daisy suit. "You obstructed me once. And paid a hellish price. You shall know only oblivion this time."

"Whether the stone hits the pitcher or the pitcher hits the stone, it's going to be bad for the pitcher," Daisy slurred.

The Quixote lunged toward me, the jackknife raised.

A gun shot exploded.

I rolled from the bed, grunted as keen-edged steel bit through heavy canvas and sweat-soaked flannel, glancing off my ribs in a stinging slap. I face-planted. The world spun from my grasp, black spots boiling through my vision.

The moldering bed crashed into the wall, dusting the floor with rotted wallpaper and crumbling sheetrock. I rolled to my back, gasping, agony searing my side, my right arm wrenched across my body at an impossible angle. My right knee screamed. I levered my left leg, dug my boot heel into the splintered wood and drove myself toward the wall and the coal oil lantern sputtering near the corner.

The Quixote towered over me, wildfire storming his gaze. He snagged my jacket lapels, dragged me to his face. Putrid spittle flecked his ashen lips, his sulfurous breath stuffing rancid fingers down my throat.

I gagged, my strength gone, pain flogging my unhinged shoulder and knee. Steaming sanguine oil slicked my side, soaked the waistband of my slacks. My vision swam, starless fireflies dancing through the fluttering light.

Another gunshot pounded into the room.

The Quixote jerked forward a step, the jackknife flying from his grasp. Howling, he flung me away, spun to face Daisy's corpse.

I slammed into the floor and rolled into the wall, limp and boneless beside the lantern.

A sickening snap and pop shook the walls.

Daisy's headless body crumpled into a fleshy lump.

The Quixote turned, dropped her head. It thumped against the floor. He stepped toward me. I shoved myself against the wall, left hand grasping the handle of the lantern, and flung it at him. He slithered from its path. Glass shattered, spewing coal oil and fire against the wall behind him. Flames licked at the oil, grasping and clawing at the floor and wall, tugging itself up ratty and tattered wallpaper and painted drywall, gorging itself in a fiery feeding frenzy.

The Quixote towered over me, his shadow blotting out the rabid firestorm rippling over the sagging ceiling. My left hand reached out, grasped the handle of the Quixote's jackknife as he yanked me from the floor. I rammed the blade through his chin to the hilt. He grunted, tossed me across the room. I crashed into the corner beside the open door, gawked at Daisy's headless corpse sprawled beside me, Danni's service weapon clutched in her festering hand.

Slimy black smoke boiled through the room, sucking the air from my chest. The doorway beside me vanished. I slumped over, scrabbled numb fingers over split and splintered wood, found Daisy's oozing and bubbling hand and the firearm clutched in her lifeless fingers.

The Quixote materialized from the roiling gray-black hurricane, the jackknife clenched in his fist. His dead eyes blazed with malevolence.

The fire roared, littered the floor with bits of charred wood and plaster from the ceiling, their blackened edges glowing orange and red. The bed burst into flames, the wood frame exploding, spewing flaming slivers and splinters through the smoke-choked air.

He stooped to grasp my coat collar, the jackknife raised. I yanked the gun from Daisy's dead grip and fired.

The Quixote howled as he staggered back into the flames. Greedy yellow-orange, undulating fingers snagged his boots and pant cuffs, grasped and clawed over boot leather, tugging themselves up ratty and tattered denim, gorging themselves in a fiery feeding frenzy. The black duster boiled and blistered, scorching the leather, glowing embers scattering through the firestorm as he twisted in torment, screaming.

The book clawed its way out from the roasting duster, dropped to the floor at the Quixote's feet. Flames licked the leather binding. The covers hissed and sizzled. Wildfire slurped the pages inside. Their edges curled and blackened, the paper evaporating into gray-black smoke.

A dissonant screech shattered the snapping thunder of the flames.

"Maggie," I wheezed, my voice trampled beneath the stampeding hooves of the roaring flames.

Coughing and choking, I used Danni's gun as leverage to drag myself from the room, clawed my broken body toward the wall. I sat up against it, watching the sooty smoke seethe through the bedroom doorway, the roiling plumes bubbling to the ceiling. They rolled across the disintegrating plastered drywall, filling the hall with scalding thunderheads.

A shadowed form appeared at the top of the stairs.

I squinted into the dark, dusty haze, my hand tightening around the butt of the gun.

The apparition walked toward me, manifested into Maggie.

She stopped when she saw me, her face twisting into a snarling mask, dripping hatred and malice.

"Maggie?"

"I hate you!" she screeched and launched herself at me, fingers hooked into talons. She leaped into me, clawing and scraping, tearing bloody trenches down my arms.

I dropped the gun, fought to control her rabid attack. She raked my face with her nails, plowed furrows down my cheeks, bit my hand when I grabbed a mauling arm. Agony lacerated my right shoulder, jolted through my neck and into the back of my skull.

"Maggie!" I pleaded. "It's Mommy! Stop!"

"I hate you," she shouted at me. "I hate you. I hate you. I hate you!" She wrenched her arm free of my grip, pummeled my face and chest with rage-hardened fists.

Desperation grabbed and shook me to my core. I grabbed her dress collar, the coarse, homespun fabric scraping my hand where Maggie had bitten me, shoved her an arm's length away, and slapped her across her face. Her head snapped sideways. She crumpled against me. I hugged her to me, tears streaming down my cheeks, my chest shuddering with each sobbing breath as I breathed her name into her knotted and matted hair.

I prayed to a God I didn't know if I believed in that she would be okay. That she was mine again. That He and Maggie would forgive me for what I had just done to try to bring my daughter back.

Smoke slithered down the walls, churned into the spaces between the walls. The bedroom doorway glowed red, the flames chewing past the blackened wood frame and melted bedroom walls.

Stomping footsteps tramped up the stairs.

Trembling, Maggie pressed herself against my chest. I retrieved Danni's gun and pointed it at the stairs.

Danni McMillan emerged from the darkness, dragging his left foot behind him. He stopped, his gaze focused on the gun clasped in my shaking hand. He leaned against the wall, panting, face swollen and bloody, one eye bloated closed.

"Emmie?"

"McMillan?"

He slogged toward us, collapsed to his knees. "We need to get the hell out of Dodge."

I shoved Maggie into his arms.

He frowned, glanced at the conflagration marching from the bedroom and back at me, uncertainty scraping his face.

The house shuddered.

Debris rained from the ceiling, writhed through the garbage strewn over the floor. Miniature campfires sprang to life.

"This isn't up for debate," I said. "Take Maggie. I'm right behind you."

The house groaned. The bedroom wall crumbled. A roaring horde of fiery fingers surged through the widening breach. Smoke charged out, eating the oxygen from the air.

"Go!" I pushed him. "Now!"

A breath of hesitation.

"I'm coming back for you." He hauled himself to his feet, vanished into the thickening mass.

I tried to stand, collapsed into the wall, began scrabbling across the floor toward the stairs.

A high-pitched squealing shriek echoed through the house.

I looked back.

The Quixote stood in the hall, his body black and bubbling like a roasting marshmallow. He gripped the burning remains of his book in his hands, the covers and pages seared nearly to ash. He stumbled toward me, dead eyes burning with their own firestorm, scorched lips muttering.

An image tugged my memories.

The Tall Man standing over the body of my mommy, a book held out to me, the blank page whispering my name, calling, promising peace and serenity.

I screamed, raised the pistol, and fired.

The Quixote and his book burst apart.

A hand grasped my shoulder. Lips touched my ear. "We need to go."

"Maggie," I cried.

"She's safe."

I wilted into his clutching grip.

He muscled me under control, pulled me down the stairs. Smoke and flames slithered after us, licking and chewing wood.

I choked and coughed, fell as he dumped me from the last step, heaving breath in the gathering charcoal-laden air and smoke. He huffed himself to his feet, yanked me in his wake, sooty smoke billowing, heat and flame scraping the room.

The house puked us from the front door, spewing smoke and ash after us. We lurched down the deck steps, trudged through mountain ranges of snow to Danni's cruiser.

He dumped me in beside Maggie, piled in to the other side, and fired the engine to life.

I found Daugherty's journal lying on the seat, curled my hand around the weathered leather binding, burned fingers brushing the ragged edge of my torn page, as I hugged Maggie to my chest, watching my childhood home collapse into a pile of ash and charred wood, the remains of the Quixote, and his book.

Emerson Daugherty

RUBY CREEK, COLORADO—JANUARY 5, 2025

Frozen late morning sunlight painted a stark blue-white path through a cloud-dusted sky. A gentle breeze tickled the barren branches of the aspens lining the narrow, winter-iced road wandering through the center of the Ruby Creek Memorial Cemetery. The stiff air smelled crisp and clean, tasted like a chilled sangria on a hot summer afternoon. Crows strutted down the center of the road, pecking the asphalt and gossiping while enjoying a brunch buffet.

I stood at the foot of two freshly filled graves, my right leg braced and my right arm slung across my chest. Maggie clasped my hand in hers, and I buried both deeply into my coat pocket. She fidgeted in the cold, her frosty breath spitting swirling clouds. She looked up at me, impatience scribbled across her face, lips pinched. She blinked the sunlight from her eyes, opened her mouth.

I looked down and frowned at her, shook my head, asking for a little more patience.

She grimaced, shifted from foot to foot, settled into an uneasy peace.

I squeezed her hand. She smiled and settled her head against my hip, a hushed sigh skipping from between her lips.

Danni McMillan leaned against the side of his cruiser behind us, hands stuffed into his jacket pockets, bruised and bloodied eyes hidden behind mirrored aviator glasses. His discolored and puffy face, beginning to turn a leprous yellow-blue, languished in the biting cold.

I felt his eyes on the back of my head, wished again that he'd accompanied Maggie and me to Sam's and Daisy's gravesites. He'd declined my desperate invitation, his expression haunted, eyes troubled. I almost ordered him to our side, bit back my impatience and discomfort, returned my attention to the dead lying in repose before us.

Grief and sadness for Sam Pellerman pricked my heart. He'd been a good man. Flawed, but he'd taught me what I needed to know to survive, despite my recalcitrance and unwillingness to listen.

"Goodbye, Sam Pellerman," I whispered into the morning chill. "Thank you for everything you tried to do for me and tried to teach me. I owe you our lives."

"Goodbye, Grampa Sam," Maggie said, her voice a hushed melody caressing my own words of farewell. "I wish that I could have gotten to meet you. And that we could have gone swimming together."

My lips trembled as a stray tear rolled down my cheek.

"Can we go now?" Maggie asked. "I'm cold."

"In a minute, baby girl. We still have to say goodbye to Gramma Daisy."

Maggie frowned, lips pouting in concentration. A heartbeat later, she grinned, her face beaming with little girl delight.

"Goodbye Gramma bi—"

"Maggie!" I rattled her arm. "We don't say that word here. It isn't respectful."

"But, Mommy," Maggie complained. "It's what you called her all the time. She grinned up at me, six-year-old devilish delight glinting from her eyes.

"Well...yes. But...Never mind," I said. "I think Gramma Daisy will understand if we just go."

We turned to leave.

The feverish stench of an acrid breath brushed past me, raising the hackles on the back of my neck. I stumbled, trembling as the daylight faded.

The image of a tall, lanky man with a gaunt face clutching a neatly trimmed salt-and-pepper beard and matching, drooping mustaches that caressed slender, pale, colorless lips ghosted my mind. A keen-edged nose sliced through the center of the mustaches, rising to grasp the calloused seam separating a pair of dead eyes that glowed crimson in the faltering light.

The lips parted, dribbling a single whispered name: "Dulcinea."

I bit the inside of my cheek.

Daylight returned.

I stared over my shoulder, peered past the skeletal trees sprouting from the frozen field. The remnants of a shadow evaporated, left behind a black stain that dimmed the air, before it too faded.

"Everything okay?"

I jumped, gaped into Danni's denim-blue eyes. I nodded. "Yeah, everything's great. Let's get out of here." He twitched an uncertain smile, took my arm, and led us back to his car.

Twisted Tales of Familiar Faces

If you enjoyed this bone-chilling retelling of the *Don Quixote* tale, don't miss out on the rest of this horrifying collection!

Humbug (Scrooge) - Andre Gonzalez

Sweethaven (Popeye) - RJ Clark

Timber Beast (Paul Bunyan) - A.K. Hughey

Alice (Alice in Wonderland) - Audrey Brice

Wish (Aladdin) - Courtney Konstantin

Quixote (Don Quixote) - Stephen Wertzbaugher

Arturius (King Arthur) - A.K. Hughey

Steamboat (Steamboat Willie) - Courtney Konstantin

Strangled (Rapunzel) - Stephen Wertzbaugher

Dethroning Oz (Wizard of Oz) - Audrey Brice

Scorned (Hercules) - Z.S. Diamanti

Check out the entire collection at www.m4lpublishing.com

Join our newsletter to stay up to date with all upcoming releases at www.m4lpublishing.com

Author's Note

This story would not have been written without the unwavering love and creative support of my wife, Kathy Wertzbaugher, to whom I owe a tremendous debt of gratitude. I would also like to thank my kids, Christine, Courtney, and Jeff, for their constant badgering, which kept me banging away at the keyboard, especially when the words didn't want to come.

A special thanks to my publisher, M4L Publishing, for their invitation to write for the Twisted Tales line, their belief in me during the dark times, and their support throughout the writing, editing, and publishing process.

Thanks to my editor, Nan Sampson Bach, who fearlessly goes where even angels fear to edit. Thanks to my writing coach, Audrey Hughey, for her continued support and tough love. And thanks to my Writing Mastermind Group, whose continuous words of encouragement and safe space allowed me to unburden my writer's soul without fear of judgment.

Enjoy this book?

We hope you enjoyed this release from M4L Publishing.

Reviews are the most helpful tools in getting new readers for any books. We don't have the financial backing of a New York publishing house and can't afford to blast our books on billboards or bus stops.

(Not yet!)

That said, your honest review can go a long way in helping us reach new readers. If you've enjoyed this book, we'd be forever grateful if you could spend a couple minutes leaving it a review (it can be as short as you like) on the site you purchased this book from.

Thank you so much!

About the author

Stephen Wertzbaugher has been fascinated with telling stories since the 3rd grade when he built a diorama and told the story of Doctor Doolittle to kindergarten classes. He wrote his first short story for an 8th grade English assignment about a coup of the US government using clones of key cabinet members. His true epiphany for spinning yarns came after seeing Star Wars in 1978 and remarking, "I want to tell stories like that."

A few decades later, he's living his dream, writing tales of horror, and urban and dark fantasy that allow him to chew on his worst fears.